RAINBOW INN

RAINBOW INN

J. SUMMERS

SAPPHIRE BOOKS

SALINAS, CALIFORNIA

Rainbow Inn
Copyright © 2015 by **J. Summers** All rights reserved.

ISBN - 978-1-939062-85-7

Book Designer- LJ Reynolds

Sapphire Books
Salinas, CA 93912
www.sapphirebooks.com

Printed in the United States of America
Second edition – February 2015

This and other Sapphire Books titles can be found at
www.sapphirebooks.com

Acknowledgments

Many people helped me write The Rainbow Inn. Thanks to our thousands of hotel guests whose constant inspiration and stories feed my writing. They will keep the stories coming and keep my creative juices flowing. Credit goes to Jan Hurley, expert proofreader, editor, and reality checker. Extra love and thanks to my soul mate and partner Denise, who continues to share my life and experiences at Casitas Laquita Hotel in beautiful Palm Springs, California. Special thanks to my publisher and good friend Roxanne Jones. Without her web eBook store L-Book.com, you would not be reading this book.

Chapter One

KIM FOR GOD's sake get out of bed. We have lots to do to get ready for Jill Carter's birthday. The guests will be arriving in three hours."

"Come on, Katie, don't be such a pain. You get so carried away with these events. You would think by now you would know how perfect you manage to make these parties." Kim was tempted to roll over and snuggle down in the covers for a while longer but the look on her lover's face told her it would be best to get moving. "Okay, I will get my ass out of bed and help like a good inn keeper. Can I at least read the paper and have a cup of coffee? Need time to get the old bones moving."

"Old? Would you stop it? You are a young woman. Stop complaining," Katie replied with a look that let Kim know she was mostly teasing.

"All right I'm coming, but I still need the coffee. Will you join me or are you going to make me feel guilty?" Kim asked.

"Of course, I'll join you. I'm sorry I'm in such a tizzy, but you know how I can be." Katie leaned down and punctuated her words with a light kiss to her lover's lips.

"Mmm. You know, honey, life is about taking some time for yourself. You should try it some time. How about right now?" Kim challenged with a raised brow. One tug on Katie's hand had her lying half beside and half on Kim. "Now this is more like it," Kim said as she pulled the smaller woman close and placed several kisses in a row along Katie's jaw before finally reaching her lips.

Katie pulled back so that she could look Kim in the face. Every time she looked into her lover's warm brown eyes she saw amazing love reflected there. She was tempted to give in to some of that personal time but there was too much yet to be done for the party, so instead she caressed Kim's face with her fingertips and smoothed the brunette strands of hair away from her face.

"It isn't that I want to rush around like a chicken with its head cut off...I just know we need to expect the unexpected, be ahead of the game, all that stuff I learned in the hotel business," Katie said with a hint of sadness.

"This isn't the Ritz Carlton. It's a small inn. Just chill out for once," Kim said perhaps a bit to brusquely. "Can't I even get a real good morning kiss?" Kim immediately regretted her words when she saw the hurt expression that settled on her lover's face. *Oops that look says I've gone too far...again.* "I'm done...you win. I'll hop in the shower." Kim knew she should probably leave well enough alone but she couldn't resist one last attempt to lure Katie into some playtime. "Want to join me? We can slip and slide all over one another!" Kim teased as she raised her eyebrows playfully and attempted to pull Katie in for a real kiss.

"No, the phone might ring. You go ahead." Not in the mood for teasing, Katie was curt in her reply as she pulled away and rolled to her feet to stand beside the bed.

"Spoilsport. I'll be done in a snap...you just carry on without me," Kim said as she left the comfort of their bed and headed for the bathroom.

"What else is new? This hotel sure takes the fun out of romance and sex, at least with each other?" Katie complained aloud to herself as she cast a glance at her retreating lover.

❧ ❧ ❧ ❧ ❧

Moments later Kim stood under the warm soothing spray of the shower with her thoughts grumbling along. *Is that the phone ringing? I can't even take a damn shower without the doorbell or phone ringing or the housekeeper barging in. What's a girl to do when Maria-full-of-life runs around the house greeting you with big hugs and kisses...naked or not she doesn't care. Guess we should start getting up at dawn? Better not even think that too loudly. Katie would jump at the chance of starting her day at dawn. At least now we sleep until seven.*

"Katie, did you get the phone?" Kim called from the shower.

"I'm getting it, but I wonder who is calling this early? I bet it's one of the guests wanting to check in before noon," Katie called back.

Katie will handle them. I need to get my clothes on fast and get this day started. We have so much to do.

Dressing as quickly as possible, she rushed to find Katie and lend a hand. "Hey, Katie, it's your turn for the shower. Too bad it will be alone," she teased as she entered the room. "Who was on the phone? Anything I can do?"

"No, I'll handle them. You just get into the kitchen and start the baking. Remember the birthday group loved the chocolate cakes you made them last year." Katie reminded.

"How do you remember what cakes I made?" *I swear she has a computer for a brain.* "I can barely remember the guests' names let alone what cakes they liked."

"Could it be that I have a computer for a brain?" Katie teased.

Kim looked up in surprise. *How does she do that?* But before she could make a comment, Katie was racing along outlining their duties for the day.

"It will take me about an hour to do the baking. Think you can get the rooms ready while I bake? Sound like a fair deal?" Kim asked.

Kim knew the kitchen was the best place to be. Room setup was awful. Each room in the inn was equipped with a full kitchen which never failed to cause an inventory nightmare. Something was always missing. But Katie seemed to be able to get the rooms perfect every time. She was wonderful. That was just one of the many ways the women complemented each other in life and in business.

"Don't think for a minute that I don't know what you're thinking. If you weren't so good in the kitchen I'd send you off to deal with these rooms in a heartbeat," Katie said.

Knowing when it was a smart to back down Kim was quick in her response. "I think I will stick to the baking. Mrs. Fields look out."

Katie left the room shaking her head but with a smile teasing at her lips.

❧❧❧❧

More than an hour later Katie was still out on the grounds checking and double checking the rooms leaving Kim to finish up the baking and deal with the phone.

As Kim worked, her hands became coated in the cake batter she was turning into the delicious concoction her guests had come to expect. Just as she was about to pour the last of the batter into prepared baking pans, it happened...the phone began to ring. She looked first at the annoying instrument where it rested on the counter a few feet away and then at her hands. "Wouldn't you know it, the phone is ringing and my hands are white with cake batter...oh well what's a little sticky stuff on the phone," she grumbled as she moved to silence the insistent ringing.

"Good morning this is Kim. How can I help you?" she answered in her best inn keeper's voice. When she heard who was on the line, her thoughts began to race almost as rapidly as her heart. *Oh shit it's Jill Carter. God, I love her.* The lesbian movie producer spent her birthdays at The Rainbow every year. This would be her sixth year at the inn. *I wish Katie had phone duty. I am so bad with the guests. Too bad she got me!*

"Hi, Jill, looking forward to seeing you today. What can I do for you this morning?...Yes, the cake has been ordered. It will be here this afternoon. The caterer is arriving at ten thirty this morning and yes it's the same lovely babe you had last year. She is on top of everyone...I mean *thing*. Yes, I told her to prepare your very special salad with all the nuts and that really creamy dressing you like." Kim answered one question after another for the woman.

"I'm baking the chocolate cakes you liked right now, hot and fresh from the oven. Mouth watering good. You can taste the moist white cake dripping with cinnamon sugar swirled between the soft layers." She laughed at the comment the woman made at the image her description created and decided to take a step further. "Finger licking good," she flirted with a lecherous laugh and then laughed even harder when she received the expected comment. Knowing that she was probably pushing things too far Kim brought her mind back to the matters at hand.

"The flowers you ordered will be here on time. I believe you wanted long stem roses, eight dozen in Waterford crystal vases. I know you gave them to your special guests when they left last year. Is that all I can help you with?" Kim asked.

"No? A stripper? You have hired a stripper?" *Oh my God, Katie is gonna freak.* "Jill, can I call you back? I need to talk to Katie about this added attraction. Give me twenty minutes or so. Is that all right?"

Kim wanted to go in search of Katie immediately to break the news to her, but she came to her senses and decided to finish the cakes first. As she worked she thought about how to best approach the subject with Katie. Jill was a good customer and had sent them a lot of business through the years. They always tried to accommodate her requests but this one just might be too much for Katie. It turned out that by the time Kim finished with the baking Katie found her. She didn't even allow Katie to take a breath before she jumped into an account of her conversation with Jill.

"God, I'm glad you came in I was just going to find you. Jill called. I did my best to review the details of her party or at least the ones I could remember. We got to the end of the conversation...at least I thought it was over till she hit me with this. She has hired a stripper this year. I didn't know what to say to her? What do you think? We have never had a stripper at the inn. Is it against the law? What kind of strip will she do? Take all of her clothes off?" Kim rushed hardly bothering to draw a breath.

"It's okay, Kim, calm down. I'm sure Jill wouldn't do anything that would be against the law? I'll give her a call and see what she has to say while you finish up the baking."

"Now I know why you always expect the unexpected. Good luck. Find out if she's doing lap dances," Kim said with a wink. "If she is, I am not leaving the room for a second. Both of us will need to be there just in case something really wild happens. It is our job to keep everyone under control." Kim struggled to keep a straight face.

"Whatever," Katie said as she rolled her eyes in response to her partner's antics.

"You do know that I'm mostly serious, right?"

"Don't fret until we have to. It never fails, Kim, you need to fret even if you don't have reason. Stay calm. I'm sure this will work out just fine," Katie assured her lover.

❧❧❧❧

A short while later, Katie took a deep breath as she picked up the phone and prepared to deal with the woman responsible for all the activity at the inn that day.

"Wish me luck," she said to her partner who stood close by.

Kim gave her a thumbs up just as the woman came on the line.

"Jill, it's Katie. Kim tells me you have added a new entertainer to your birthday celebration this year, a stripper," Katie began the conversation.

She wasn't necessarily against the idea but there were some questions their guest would need to answer.

"I've got a few questions if you wouldn't mind? Who is she and what is she planning to do besides stripping?" Katie asked as she released a sigh. "Exactly how much does she take off?" and then paused for the answer. "Oh really? That much? Jill, please make sure we keep this under control. You have been a great guest, and we wouldn't want anything to change our relationship. Will you please have Suzie...Bella or whatever her name is give us a call? We'd like to speak to her before she arrives." Katie squeezed her eyes closed for a second. "We'll see you later. Bye for now," she ended the call.

"Kim, I hate this," she said as she turned to her

partner.

"Katie, we could say *no*."

"I know, but my gut feeling says it will be okay," Katie replied.

"Then let's go with your gut," Kim offered her support. "The party is stressful enough with all the Hollywood types and the egos. Add a stripper to the mix, anything can happen. And it will if I know Jill and her group. Paris Hilton watch out. Jill Carter is bringing a stripper. The Rainbow will never be the same. I thought last year was off the wall. Do you remember the girl Jill brought with her? She was beautiful. Long legs, small behind, long blonde hair. I remember it cascaded down her back stopping right at the crack of her tiny white butt."

"I didn't know you paid so much attention to those details," Katie challenged.

"How could you miss them? Oh, I forgot you were way too busy chatting with Jill reviewing all the details of each and every event that was to happen during the day to even notice the beauties around the pool," Kim said.

"Someone has to work around here," Katie replied.

"A person can work and look. Even when I'm playing and singing in the cellar, I am always looking. It's never stopped me from singing and playing. Can't you work and look at the same time? I remember your little eyes straying when that number strolled past you last weekend. You spent far too much time talking to her by the pool. In fact, every time I saw you that day you were hanging by her side. Not that I'm jealous, just reminding you I am not the only one who looks. Guess it comes with the territory."

"Kim, if you are surrounded by women, what's your choice?"

"Good, glad you agree...glad we have Jill under

control for now. I was worried she would spring another surprise on us."

"Don't be so sure she won't."

"I can hardly wait to see what long-legged babe she'll have on her arm this year. Must be hard working around all those actresses all day long and not be tempted to have your way with all of them. Guess that's why she never stays with one person for more than a party. I'm sure she calls them all baby. Keeps from embarrassing moments during sex. 'Oh, baby...sure feels good, baby...oh please do it more, baby.'"

"Okay, Kim, that's enough I get the picture."

"Katie, is that why you call me *baby*?" Kim teased.

"Kim, get a life. Come on we have loads to do before noon." Before either woman could move they heard the buzzer indicating someone was at the gate.

"Will you please answer the gate, *baby*?" Katie asked with a wink. "It must be the caterer or the flowers."

"I'm on my way." *Buzz...buzz. For God's sake whoever it is has zero patience.* "Okay, I'm coming."

"Hi, where do you want these?" the delivery clerk asked.

"Flowers? Come on follow me. We'll put them in Room 31 for now. Do you have the vases?" Kim asked.

"What vases? I don't have an order for any vases just the roses," the delivery man replied.

"I specifically ordered Waterford vases. I gave your order taker a deposit for twenty Waterford vases."

"You know we cannot get that many or even one Waterford vase today. They are a special order," he explained.

Kim felt her blood pressure begin to elevate as she lost patience with the man. "That isn't my problem. It's yours. You screwed up the order, not me."

"Well, Missy, I can't do a thing about the vases. You need to go to Macy's to see if they have twenty," he replied in an equally frustrated tone.

"What! Are you a nutcase? Macy's wouldn't stock twenty friggin Waterford vases, no way. You are worthless. Just get out of here." *Shit, shit now what are we going to do. I should have checked on the order days ago instead of assuming they would get it right. Now all I need is for the caterer to forget something. Katie is going to give me hell for not reviewing this order weeks ago. I have told her time and again you can't trust me with these details. May as well get it over with and face the music.* "Katie, we have a big problem."

"What is it, Kim? Forget to order vases for the flowers?"

"How did you know?"

"You know I can never trust you to check on or follow up on anything. You are always way too busy on the computer or planning our next vacation to remember to check on business details. Which, by the way, allows us to go on those wonderful vacations. I had the forethought to call the florist myself weeks ago. He told me he would have to charge a bundle of money for the vases. I ordered them from a distributor who got them for me at a greatly reduced price," Katie explained.

"Why didn't you tell me? I just made the delivery guy's weenie really small. He will never deliver here again," Kim said with crestfallen look.

"Don't worry. Delivery guys come and go. Here today, gay delivery guy, gone tomorrow," Katie said as she stifled a laugh. "Chill out. At least we don't have to go to a retail store and buy twenty vases. Right?"

"Yes, Katie, you are always right. Go on, break the news. What have you changed about the catering order?

Anything I should know about?"

"No, my darling, nothing," Katie assured her repentant partner.

"Good. I can go to the door without ripping Mary's head off. Not that I would do such a thing to such a beautiful specimen. Mary is some eye candy." Kim pretended to wipe drool from the corner of her mouth.

"Kim, stop the fantasizing and drooling, time for that later," Katie chastised. But her grin let Kim know she was just teasing.

"Sure, dear," Kim replied in her best henpecked voice.

❧ ❧ ❧ ❧

"Katie, do you know where Darla is?" Kim asked some time later. "The morning has gone by so fast I hardly missed her."

"I think she's at the gym or taking her morning bike ride. Haven't seen her yet this morning. Darla is such a studette...swimming, biking, the gym...what a gal. Remember when she landed on our doorstep ten years ago?" Kim asked.

"Yeah, I do. She has been a lifesaver over the years—don't know what we would do without her? Don't you agree, Kim?"

"Yes, of course. Our lives are much easier with Darla around. She allows us to get away from this place once in a while. Not to mention she is very handy in the garden. The guests just love her. Some love her way too much," Kim added with a roll of her eyes.

"Don't forget she is a wonderful comedian, and she does front your shows. The costumes she comes up with! I think we should have her strip for Jill's party before you and Donna start to play. She will give the real stripper a run for her money, besides Jill will just love the show," Katie said.

"Are you serious? Because if you are, I'm sure Darla will go for it," Kim said with a hopeful expression.

"Go for it, *baby!*"

"Okay, hon. I will find Darla and tell her she is on for Saturday night's entertainment."

⁂

Kim stopped off at the pool on her way to find Darla. She needed to have a word with the poolman to be sure everything was ready for their guests.

"Vic, good morning. The pool will be full this weekend because we have a big party. They will be in the pool playing games all weekend. I would guess beer will be a big part of the poolside activities. I'm hoping the food stays out of the pool."

"Sure, Kim I will make sure the pool is perfect. Sophie and I are headed to Mexico this weekend. Guess you and Katie have your hands full and can't make it."

"I wish we could. No rest for us. It's a big party with wild people. We have all we can do to stay on top of the activities–whatever they may be. You and Sophie have a good time for us. Drink a few margaritas at La Fonda."

⁂

After her brief conversation with Vic, it didn't take long for Kim to locate Darla.

"Darla, I need to talk to you after you wind down from your bike ride."

"Okay, Kim, I will come find you in a few minutes.

Let me take a shower first."

"Sure, see you in a few."

Darla will be up for this show I'm sure. She's always ready for a dress up for a drag moment. I sometimes wonder where she comes up with the personas. Never know who she is going to be. This time I want her to be a stripper. Jill will love it. I know Darla will be in her element. Any excuse to take her clothes off in public. Donna and I will provide the strip music...it will be great. Katie will be livid. She hates this kind of behavior, but she did tell me to go for it. I won't tell her exactly what is happening, let it be a surprise. I will get shit afterwards...oh well, Jill will be pleased. I know the hired stripper will be worse than Darla. I think?

※ ※ ※ ※

As promised Darla showed up at Kim's side a short while later.

"Hey, Darla, thanks for finding me. Did you have a good ride?" Kim asked.

"Yes, I went about twenty miles."

"Good God, girl. What's up with that?"

"I need the exercise. You know we aren't getting any younger, have to keep these muscles in shape...need to look good in my bathing suit for the young lesbians," Darla replied as she pointed to her body.

"Darla, you don't have to compete with those g-strings."

"Kim, you know most of the time when you think I'm reading my book by the pool with my dark glasses on, I'm actually peering over them gazing at those nice tight buns parading around the pool. Better yet, those plump butts floating on the mats just wet enough to make those buns sparkle under the sun's glow," she said with a lecherous grin.

"Speaking of butts and buns, you know Jill is arriving this afternoon with her group?" Kim turned the conversation to the real reason she needed to talk with Darla.

"Yes, I know. What a bunch," Darla laughed.

"Jill informed us she has hired a stripper for the party."

"What?"

"Yes, a stripper," Kim assured her.

"She will rain on my parade."

"No, that is what I want to talk to you about. I've had a change of plans. I want you to strip," Kim told her and quickly got the response she expected.

"Well, of course. That sounds like fun," Darla said with enthusiasm.

"I thought you would enjoy the chance to show off your many talents," Kim said with a wink.

"You know it will take me all day to get ready. I have to go to Q Trading and Tommy Rose's store for the perfect dress or dresses. Can I have the charge card please?" Darla asked.

"Don't spend too much money," Kim cautioned.

"I won't. I can get everything I need for under a hundred dollars. Is that okay?"

"Sure. Please don't tell Katie until after it's all over. She's not going to be happy with us. You know how she can be?"

"Yes, she hates it when the two of us get together. It always means money."

"Darla, Katie might need your help this afternoon with the caterer so don't be gone too long."

"I won't. Can I borrow the car?" Darla asked.

"Sure."

Damn, there's the door bell ringing. It has to be the caterer this time. Darla missed her chance to help. I know how much she enjoys Beth...everyone loves Beth. Her cooking is wonderful, and she's not bad on the eyes. Beth has been serving the lesbian community for several years. You can't walk into a party without seeing Beth.

"Katie, I'll get the door, it must be Beth," Kim called as she moved to open the door.

"Hola, mi bonita chiquita," Beth greeted her.

"Beth, what's with the Espanola?"

"Kim, didn't you know the theme of Jill's party is a trip to Old Mexico?" Beth asked.

No, hadn't a clue. Just like Jill...another surprise. Guess the stripper will be a cute little tan Mexican girl with long dark flowing hair, big brown eyes. "I can't wait. Beth what do you need me to do for you?"

"Nothing right now, I want to turn Casitas Laquita into the old Mexican hacienda of its past. Good idea Jill has. The grounds will come alive with music and fiesta; the landscaping and the architecture are all here. I just need to fluff it up a bit."

"You go ahead and fluff, Beth, while I daydream about Mexico. Katie and I could be in Mexico right now."

❧❧❧❧

"Katie, Beth is here fluffing for Jill's party. I talked to Darla she is ready to help entertain. I think everything is under control. I know you will need to review every detail. I'm sure I have forgotten something," Kim told her partner.

"Sure, my love, I will before Jill and her group arrive. Would you please go and run the arrival reports? I need to recheck the folios, see who's with whom. You know how lesbians switch partners. We have a bad habit of moving one out and another right in. We should have been in the U-Haul business."

"Don't be silly. We have a few very good friends who have been together many years. Our business welcomes so many guests each year we are bound to see the good, bad and the ugly. Lucky for us it has been mostly good."

"Katie said. Good girl. Keep up the positive thinking. I will go run your reports be back in a few."

"Hurry, it is almost noon. Jill will be cruising up at any second," Kim requested.

"I will be right back...stop fretting," Katie said as she gave her partner and encouraging squeeze on the shoulder as she passed.

❧❧❧❧

Katie was distracted from preparations when Maria came running into the room talking rapidly in Spanish.

"Maria what's wrong? Stop yelling and speak English, slow down."

"Miss Katie, please come quick. Something is wrong with Room 28."

"Maria, what is wrong?"

"Come I will show you."

This can't be happening. Jill will be arriving in a few minutes all we need is a backed up toilet, a flood, or a broken something. I hope whatever it is Kim can fix it fast.

"Miss Katie, look no water...the room has no water," Maria said as she turned the faucets back and forth.

"This is not a good thing," Katie replied as she tried not to panic. "Maria, have you checked to see if any of the rooms have water?"

"I don't know. I will go check next door."

"What would be worse – no water in one room or the entire side of the hotel without water?" Katie questioned herself.

"Room 29 has no water," Maria informed her upon her return.

What is this? God must be mad at us.

"Maria run fast. Go get Kim. Bring her back here," Katie instructed.

Maria made a beeline for the house yelling,"Miss Kim come quick. Miss Katie needs you right away."

The woman was in such a tizzy by the time she found Kim, she was once again difficult to understand and short of breath.

"Calm down, Maria, what's the big rush?" Kim asked.

"No water...the room has no water"

"What do you mean no water?" *Oh, hell she doesn't know anything. I need to see for myself.*

Kim went straight to the rooms in search of Katie to find out what was going on. It only took her a few minutes to arrive at her partner's side.

"Katie, what is happening?"

"If I knew what was happening, I would not have sent for you," Katie said. "There's not any water in the rooms. I checked the other rooms while Maria went to get you. Nothing. We don't need this. Not today."

"I know, honey. This is terrible timing. We'll figure it out. The first thing that comes to my mind is a broken water main. I hope it isn't here on the property. Maybe the city is fixing something in the neighborhood. Whatever is going on we need to find out now. Jill will have a fit if she doesn't have water. I will walk the property, see if I can find a big wet puddle or maybe a lake," Kim attempted to lighten the mood.

"Don't be smart, Kim. This is no time to be joking around," Katie replied.

"I'm sorry, Katie. I won't make light of it anymore. Why don't you go out to the street front and back to see if you see any action like water company trucks? Meet you back in 28 in a few minutes," Kim directed.

❧❧❧❧

"Find anything?" Katie asked once they were back together.

"No lakes," Kim replied with a grin.

"How about you?"

"Not a thing," Katie said.

"I will go call the water company. They must be doing something affecting only one side of the hotel," Kim decided.

"The front gate is ringing. It must be Jill. What will I tell her?" Katie asked.

"Katie, just tell her we have a slight problem. It will be fixed in an hour. Send her to the bar for a drink on us. She can use the restroom in one of the other rooms for now," Kim suggested.

"That may be easier said than done. She will have Miss Right on her arm expecting the royal treatment. What will she get? No water in her room. Not so sure, this is going to go well," Katie worried.

Gush, splash–a burst of water suddenly surged out of every faucet including the john.

"Thank you, God, we have water!" Katie exclaimed.

"Katie, get the door. I'll clean up the water," Kim promised.

❧❧❧❧

"Jill, welcome, come in," Katie greeted their guest with a welcoming smile.

"Hello, Katie, let me introduce you to Trish," Jill replied.

"Very nice to meet you, Trish. I hope you will have a wonderful stay with us. Jill, how was the traffic from LA?" Katie asked.

"Not bad, my new car zipped along. We listened to Trish's new CD release. We'll play it for you and Kim later," Jill offered.

"Can't wait. You should talk to Kim. Maybe Trish can sit in with her and Donna, sing a few songs," Katie suggested.

"That would be terrific. Right, Trish?"

"Super, can't wait...that will be cool," Trish answered.

"Jill, Trish, this way to your room, the romance suite," Katie offered as she led them to their suite.

"Jill, the room is everything you said it would be," Trish proclaimed as she looked around the room set for romance.

"Glad you like it, Babe," Jill said as she pulled the woman in for kiss.

"I will leave you two alone to unpack and get settled. Jill, can I meet with you in a bit? We need to go over the catering and party details," Katie said.

"Katie, I need more than a bit, if you know what I mean," Jill responded as she pulled Trish in for another kiss.

"Sure, take your time. Just give me a call when you finish. I mean after you get settled," Katie said in a rush as she made a quick exit.

"Great...will call you, love," Jill said as the door

clicked shut behind Katie.

⁂

"Katie, did you get Jill and her girlfriend settled in?" Kim asked.

"Yes, I left them in their room. Jill seemed to be really hot to get started with her weekend," Katie said. "She couldn't seem to keep her hands off her."

"So how cute is the new friend?" Kim asked.

"Very nice, a singer; she wants to sit in with you and Donna," Katie said and waited for her reaction.

"That's fine as long as we know her songs."

"Kim, I have faith in you two. You can do anything. If you happen to answer the phone when Jill calls, come get me. She needs to review the weekend's events."

"I wouldn't hold your breath...it might be a long time. You know Jill is a mad woman in bed. Well...not just in bed," Kim said.

"Stop it, Kim. She is very sweet."

"Are we talking about the same person, Katie? "

"Chill out. You know Jill just loves you," Katie replied.

"I know she does. She is just so demanding," Kim said.

"Kim, this is the business, we are here to serve and provide the best experiences for our guests, no matter how tedious that might be. Service is our main goal. The Rainbow is known for excellent service," Katie reminded her lover and business partner.

"That is due to all of your hard work. You are the best with the guests. I am always amazed you have a good word for everyone, always smiling. How do you do it?"

"I love this business. It has been my life."

"Thank goodness for you, my sweetheart. That is why I love you." Kim cast a loving gaze on her partner as once again the door bell sounded.

"Hon, can you go answer the door? Another one of Jill's guests is checking in. This might be Sha. She was due right after Jill. You go smile and be nice and friendly," Katie said.

"I am friendly, just not quite as friendly as you," Kim replied.

Katie was right in her assessment. When Kim reached the door she found Sha waiting with another woman.

"Sha, good to see you and Jess. We haven't seen you since the last party. How have you been?" Kim asked as she welcomed them to the inn.

"Very busy! Jill keeps us hopping, one major picture after another, hard to get time to visit our desert retreat. I think about this place all the time. When Jill starts to lose it, I want to get in my car and drive to beautiful Palm Springs. You and Katie are so lucky; no more stress, just a beautiful place to chill," Sha said.

"Sha, it is always a pleasure to have you visit. Let me show you to your room," Kim offered. They walked down the hall towards her room and Kim unlocked the door.

"Yes, just as I remembered," Sha said with a sigh of contentment. "Oh, the bed is so soft...excuse me while I crash for a while. Come on and join me, Jess," Sha invited.

"Sha, we need to unpack," Jess responded.

"Who gives a damn about unpacking? Get your sweet little ass over here," Sha instructed.

"I will leave you two alone. See you later." Kim moved to make a hasty retreat.

"Good bye, Kim and thanks for having such a wonderful place for us," Sha called from the bed.

"It is our pleasure. We are here to please," Kim replied as she reached the door.

"Oh really? Kim, sure you don't want to join us for a little afternoon delight?" Sha questioned.

"Sha, you are a sicko. Have a good time girls. Looks like you have already started. Be careful, Sha, you might hurt the girl," Kim cautioned as she made her exit.

"Not a chance. She likes it rough."

※ ※ ※ ※

The gate rang non-stop for three hours. All of Jill's friends and business associates arrived. The hotel was full to capacity with the most gorgeous women LA could provide. The stars were out in Palm Springs.

Kim was looking around for Darla. The two of them had their hands full and the guests were beginning to show signs of restlessness. Darla had been gone for hours but the guests needed attention and they needed it now.

It was one of the curses of owning a hotel...a party every day. Katie and Kim treasured the slow quiet days when things were much calmer and they could actually get to know their customers.

On a day like this one everyone was out to impress. Jill and her gal pal were still in their room. Kim didn't expect to see them till the sun went down for the cocktail hour. Most everyone else was soaking up the sun and appeared to be having a really good time. The bathing suits and bodies were all the entertainment anyone could possibly need. Kim still hadn't gotten used to the g-strings. She and Katie made a pact never to allow nudity around the pool. After ten years in business, they had stuck to that agreement.

Just as Kim's thoughts turned to Darla, she came

rushing in.

"Darla, thank God you're back. I was beginning to wonder if you had plans to return today?"

"Kim, I couldn't help myself. It is hard trying on all those gowns, makes a girl tired, in and out of dress after dress."

"How many did you buy?" Kim asked.

"I bought three. Don't worry. Tommie said I could bring back the ones I didn't wear. He is so sweet. He didn't even charge me for the dresses, said he would settle up when I came back. I had to take advantage of the offer."

"Great...now we have lots of work to do," Kim said.

"Has everyone checked in?"

"No thanks to your help. All of them are here and ready to party. Go take a look at all the g-strings floating on the mats in the pool," Kim suggested.

"I will go change and get my ass out to the pool immediately," Darla said with a laugh.

"Darla, while you're out there gawking, please see to the poolside service, too."

"You bet, my sweet thing, I will do everything to please those little darlings."

"I just bet you will," Kim replied.

With that off her plate, Kim went to find Katie and see what they needed to get prepared for that evening's catered dinner. Beth should be arriving any time with her setup for the first fiesta. Kim thought she would have been here by now. She had brought loads of things by earlier that morning.

❦❦❦

Damn, there's the gate again. It must be Beth and her girls. Kim complained to herself as she answered the door yet again.

"Beth, come on in. The party has arrived," Kim invited.

"Where is Jill?" Beth asked.

"Jill is in bed with her newest fling."

"Oh my, I really need to speak to her," the caterer said.

"Good luck. Want me to call or go to her room and see if I can get a rise out of her?" Kim offered.

"Kim, I believe getting a rise isn't the issue," Beth offered with a suggestive grin. "Yes, please go see if we can talk to her now."

Okay here goes. When Kim got to the door all the shutters were closed. *This could be a good thing or bad. Here goes.* Kim knocked on the door and called out, "Jill are you there? Beth is here. She wants to speak to you before she starts to setup for dinner tonight" *Not a sound. I can knock again or just forget the whole thing...let Beth do whatever. Problem with that is Jill will not like whatever we decide if she wasn't part of the decision making. I will just call her phone. The woman listened for the ringing to begin on the other side of the door.*

"Yes," a voice answered. "Can I help you?"

"Jill, it's Kim."

"This better be important. I was right in the middle of some really good sex," her guest replied with obvious displeasure at being interrupted.

"Jill, Beth is here. She really needs your help with the dinner plans."

"Can't Katie take care of this?'

"Yes, she can, as long as you won't be rearranging everything at the last minute," Kim agreed.

"Sex or dinner arrangements? Right now, it's sex," Jill decided.

"Okay I'll pass this on to Katie and Beth. Have fun."

"You know I will."

※ ※ ※ ※

"Beth, Jill wants you and Katie to take full charge of the dinner plans for tonight. She is very busy right now and will be for the balance of the afternoon. Let's go get Katie. She can lend a hand," Kim informed the caterer.

She knew Katie wasn't going to be pleased with the turn of events but it was all part of the customer service they offered at the inn. The sooner she brought Katie into the picture the better.

"Katie, Beth and I just spoke to Jill. She is preoccupied for the entire afternoon, has no time to help with the dinner plans. She has asked you and Beth to proceed without her," Kim told her lover.

"You know how Jill has to be in charge. She'll hate some major thing and we will have to change things last minute," Katie complained.

"I know but she has promised she would let you two do whatever you wanted with no changes. We'll see," Kim replied.

"Beth, do you really need me?" Katie asked.

"Not really, you have your hands full. I'll take complete responsibility for the dinner. I'll get out of your hair. Please feel free to check on the progress," Beth said.

"Sure, Beth. I know you'll make this a wonderful event."

※ ※ ※ ※

The sun was casting a glow over the mountains above Palm Springs. The sky was bright blue like on a post card. The guests at The Rainbow lathered themselves with suntan lotion while sipping on cocktails that were being served by the lovely Darla. Conversations were lively, as if everyone was talking at once vying for attention.

This crowd is very animated. Think that is what Hollywood does to young lesbians? I can only relate to the L-Word. These women seemed to step right out of the last episode. Kim looked out over the group.

Jill had the party at the inn every year and each year the faces changed. Kim believed Jill ran her business partners and employees to the ground. She was a very successful producer, high energy and very smart. People either loved her or hated her. She was extremely motivated, hot tempered, never taking no for an answer.

Katie was the only one who seemed to get her. Katie had such a good personality, never let a situation get the better of her.

I sure wish I could be so calm and cool. Not me... never. I can't tell you how many times Katie has told me to get over it. One of us has to be the saint. Sure not me.

If you're in the hotel business you must have a firm but kind attitude. First it is a business even when it gets tough to tell a guest who's needing to cancel a reservation right before they are supposed to arrive that they will be charged according to the cancellation policy.

I still, after ten years, have trouble saying those words. Katie and Darla on the other hand seem to handle the situation so well. Think I will just stick to my music, computer, painting and baking breads for the guests. Keeps me out of trouble.

❧ ❧ ❧ ❧

"Sha, hi, can I help you?"

"You sure can, Kim."

"What can I do for you?"

"I really need Marilyn to come give my date and me a massage. I know this is last minute. Jess has been so wonderful the last couple of hours I can't begin to tell you the pleasure she has given me. I want her to relax and have a treat. I need her to recover for later tonight, if you know what I mean."

"Yes, Sha, I know exactly what you mean."

"Boy. Kim, she has been the best yet. I have never, ever been so in love."

"Do you mean in lust?" Kim questioned.

"Shit, you know what I mean. Just get Marilyn for me, please," Sha instructed.

"I will do my best. You know how popular she is."

"I know you can work magic, Kim. Maybe you could do the massage?"

"Not in your wildest imagination or mine for that matter."

"We will be poolside just come let us know when she will arrive."

"Do my best."

❧❧❧❧

"Hello, is this Marilyn?"

"Yes, Kim, what can I do for you this lovely afternoon?"

"I really need a favor. We have a very important group in this weekend...in fact, I think you know them."

"Refresh my memory. You know I see so many people," Marilyn said.

"I know, Marilyn, maybe if I give you a physical description that might be better than a name."

"Kim, you are such a bitch, but you're right. I see more of their bodies than their faces in my line of work."

"I'll start with the name. It's Sha and her new girlfriend, Jess. They are with Jill's group."

"Oh yes, I remember Sha. How could I forget her? One of these days, I'll tell you a really good story about Sha from LA."

"Can't wait. Sure it will be a good one."

"What does the darling want?"

"Not for her. She wants you to do her girlfriend. Can you make it this afternoon?"

"I'll clear my schedule for her any time."

"Man, Marilyn, you must have a really good story. You never clear your schedule for anyone."

"Tell the darling I will see her new squeeze at three o'clock," Marilyn said.

"Great. Thanks," Kim said in relief.

Somehow, I don't think Marilyn is doing this as a favor to me. I really need to hear the gory details about Sha and Marilyn. I know Marilyn has clients in LA and a very good following of lesbians.

Kim had gotten a massage from her a couple of times. It was wonderful but had been a long time. After a while, Kim began to feel uncomfortable with her seeing her body since they worked with her.

I should get over it, as Katie would say. Need to find Sha and give her the good news.

❧❧❧❧

"Sha, great news...Marilyn will be here at three today to work on Jess," Kim told her guest.

"Thanks. I knew you would work your magic."

"Not sure it was my magic. Somehow I think it was

yours."

"Be quiet, Kim, Jess will hear you. Don't want her to think I had anything to do with Marilyn. I want her to feel special this weekend. You know, like she is the only one. If she even thinks I have a fix on anyone else, sex will be off for the next week and that would spoil the entire weekend," Sha cautioned.

"Sure, I will keep it between us."

"You are the best ever, Kim."

❧❧❧

"Kim, Kim," a voice billowed from across the pool.

"I will be right over. Kim walked through the mass of bikini clad women finally reaching Sam. Sam, how are you? I haven't seen you in ages. I know it seems we only see you once a year. What is up with that? Don't like the hotel?"

"No, you can't even believe how busy Jill keeps me. I hardly have time to have a good date."

"Sam, what do you mean with all those gorgeous actresses around the sets you can't find a date?"

"No, not a good, long lasting, intimate date. One-night stands are in fashion when you work for Jill. She is very strict about long ongoing attachments during a movie shoot. She tells us it breeds trouble and jealousies. I think she is the one who is jealous. Jill likes all the women for herself. She stays mighty busy. I swear she has as many as three women going at a time. I just don't know how she does it, Kim," Sam lamented.

"Sam, somehow I can't see you sitting behind the scenes celibate.

It's very difficult to find more than a quickie on the set. Most of the women are bi, just out to experiment. It was fun in the beginning, not anymore; gets old after a while.

Most women envy your job jet-setting around the world meeting so many people," Kim offered.

"As I said, it gets old. I envy you and Katie. You two have such a wonderful relationship and you work together so well. I want to find what you have. How do you do it?" the woman asked.

"I guess we never think about how we do it, we just enjoy one another."

"I guess both you and Katie have taken the ego out of your relationship."

"I try not to interfere with Katie's running of the hotel, and she lets me do whatever I want."

"You go, girl. Here's to many more enjoyable years."

"Thanks, Sam. Now, can I get you anything?"

"No, I'm good. Just wanted to say hello."

"Just call if you need anything other than my wife."

❧❧❧❧

"Katie, how are things coming for tonight?" Kim asked.

"Just fine. Beth is working her tail off. The hotel, if you hadn't noticed, looks more like a Mexican Hacienda."

"You mean like Juliette's winery?"

"Yes, like the winery. I want to leave for Mexico right now," Katie said with a sigh.

"We will take a trip very soon."

"First things first, we have to make this party a success for Jill and her friends," Katie said.

"I know...business first."

"You got it."

"Katie, can I do anything?"

"Kim, the list is very long. This is the first night. You can check on Beth, see if she needs any help".

❧❧❧❧

"Beth, how are things going? Need any help?" Kim asked.

"Not right now, thanks for asking," the caterer replied as she continued to set up for the meal.

"Good, I need to go to the wine cellar and get ready for tomorrow night's performance. Beth, did I tell you Jill has a stripper coming?"

"No, you didn't tell me. I can't miss that show," Beth said with a touch of excitement.

"I don't know. You might want to miss it. Donna and I are playing after she finishes–that is if we can play?"

"Kim, a little flesh is good for the heart. Keeps it pumping."

"I'm not sure I need the excitement."

"Dear, you are showing your age."

"No, I'm worried about the cops. I believe it is against the law to have a strip show."

"Don't be silly. What's a little sex among friends? Remember the last party I catered, the Thompson party?" Beth asked.

"Yes, I remember. What happened?"

"Well, the birthday girl really loved my talents and I don't mean my cooking. We met up the following weekend in her Beverly Hills home. It was right out of a novel. She had butlers, a private chef, maids, a beautiful pool girl. I was in heaven," Beth shared.

"I knew she was rich, just wasn't sure to what extent," Kim said.

"Dana told me after a few drinks that she had been

married and the guy passed away. She inherited all of his money. She also had quite a bit of her own. We did the club scene stayed out till three in the morning. When we returned to her house we had sex on every counter top and floor in the entire house," Beth said.

"My God!"

"Think she was making up for lost female contact," Beth ignored Kim's reaction and continued her story. "Two days later I felt as if I had been run over by a truck. My entire body hurt, every inch of it. I felt pain in places no one should ever feel pain."

"I think that's enough! You have given me enough information," Kim cautioned.

"I just wanted you to know a little stripper never hurt anyone."

"Just out of curiosity, Beth, have you seen Dana Thompson again?"

"What do you think?"

"Guess you're hurting on regular basis."

"Not exactly. I've been going to the gym. Helps tone those unused muscles," Beth offered.

"Good for you. Keep pumping. I will check on Miss Buff Body later."

"Kim, want to take a look? Room 35 is empty," Beth invited.

"No, I'll pass," Kim easily replied.

"Oh come on...it could be fun," Beth tempted.

"Beth, not that I don't think you're beautiful but I don't mess around."

"I know. It is Katie sand only Katie."

"You got it. See you later."

"Kim, been looking for you, Marilyn just started a massage for Sha's new friend. Jill hasn't come out of her room all afternoon, and the other guests are getting drunk." Katie complained.

"So what else is new? I expect by dinner time no one will enjoy the dinner? I noticed the lounge chairs are quite busy; what are those women doing?"

"Think its called heavy petting. The g-strings are on the deck. I can't quite make out what is happening. Should we go look?"

"No, you are crazy. I saw Maria staring across the pool. Poor thing, our straight catholic housekeeper. What does she tell her friends about what happens at her job?"

"I would guess *nothing*. Would you?"

"No. I think they would make her quit."

"You bet they would. Thank God Vic cleans the pool early in the morning. He would really get an eyeful right now."

"He has seen a lot more. Remember he services the gay guy hotels. Can you imagine?"

"Don't want to."

Chapter Two

Dinner Is Served

Jill, it is good to finally see your smiling face," Kim said as she greeted their guest.

"I had a wonderful afternoon. Trish is the love of my life and she seems to sense my every need. I love that I don't have to ask for anything."

"I'm happy for you, Jill," Kim interrupted with a smile.

"She's so sweet and sensitive. That is very unusual for an entertainer. I've had the best of the best...the most attractive sought after actresses in Hollywood. They were loads of fun but really high maintenance. I had to be the aggressor. They just laid back and took what I gave them. Not much fun for me. This time I'm on my back taking. What a joy," Jill rambled on about her latest love.

"You sure know how to pick your women," Kim replied with a wry grin.

"I'm ready to party. How are things coming? Is Beth under control? And Katie, she must be frantic."

"No, not really, both seem to be doing just fine. The party is ready to happen."

"Guess I need to stay on my back longer? You should have told me I had more time. I might just revisit Trish. Think she is still in the mood?" Jill questioned with devilish charm.

"Ahh, Jill, how about coming with me to check and

make sure we have the gift table arranged just the way you like?" Kim asked. She wanted to keep her guest focused on the little details that needed to be ironed out. "You also must come sample Beth's food. It smells so good and Katie needs you to be sure we have the tables arranged perfectly with your favorite people sitting together.Most of the guests have over-served themselves already."

"Oh, that's perfect! That way I can say anything and they won't remember any of my nasty comments. I had planned to speak to a few key people about their promotions and if they're a bit over the edge they won't ask for more money. More work for the same pay. Need to maintain the lifestyle to which I have become accustomed. Right, Kim? Have to pay you for these parties now don't I?"

"Guess you do, Jill."

"That's my girl. Hey think Katie would mind if I hired you? I could use your talents on the road."

"She might miss me," Kim replied.

"Oh, yes, think I heard you are very good," Jill offered with a lecherous grin.

"What?"

"Yes, I believe I ran into someone who told me you're really hot," Jill teased.

"Nice to know someone thinks I'm hot. Might they be referring to my hot flashes?" Kim replied with humor.

A few minutes later Jill was surveying the set up for the party with Katie.

"Nice job, Katie. I've been chatting with your hot girl friend. She seems to have everything under control. She even managed to get Marilyn to massage Sha's new girlfriend. Marilyn dropped all her other appointments and came right over. Some service."

"We mean to please!" Katie replied in her most

polite innkeeper's voice.

"Katie, let's check the gift table," Jill said as she turned toward the table. "Did the Waterford vases arrive?"

"Yes, they did, despite a little confusion."

"Oh my table is beautiful! You have outdone yourself, Katie. I swear I was trying to hire Kim. Can I have the two of you?"

"Thank you so much, Jill, but I think we have our hands full with the hotel."

"I know but I would pay you so much more. It would be so wonderful traveling the world...seeing so many places...mingling with the rich and famous."

"You're too kind. I know you've had such a relaxing afternoon that you're just caught up in the moment," Katie responded.

"If you reconsider, you know how to find me," the producer offered.

"Yes, we sure do."

"Let's see the tables. I'll check the name tags. I don't want the bitchy women sitting next to one another," Jill said as she moved to the seating area.

Kim moved to Katie's side for quiet conversation while the woman of the hour checked the tables.

"Katie?"

"Yes, Kim."

"How did you place the names on the table?"

"Kim, you forget this is party number eight. Many of the same key players are here. I've seen Jill interact with them over the years. The only things that ever changes are the girlfriends. The newcomers I just spread around."

"You are really good. I still have trouble remembering all of the names. What would I do without you?" Kim asked.

"I don't know, guess you would manage somehow,"

Katie offered with a knowing look.

"No, I would not."

"I only changed three names," Jill said as she joined the innkeepers. "I know a couple of the women are lusting after the other person's partner. We don't need a fight tonight. If they score after dinner in their rooms so be it. I just don't want to see sparks during my wonderful dinner party. I'm off since it looks like things are under control. I think I'll go see if Trish needs help dressing? Or maybe undressing. I seem to have time on my hands. I can think of really nasty things I can do with these hands for a couple of hours," Jill said.

"You go for it, Jill."

"I will, ladies...you have fun without me."

"Kim, whose names did Jill change, just curious?" Katie asked the moment they were alone.

"I'll go look. Let's see...she moved Nancy and Teri away from Brook and Barb. I was wondering why Barb and Teri seemed to be so close all day. I thought I saw Barb touching Teri's legs. Looked like she was applying suntan lotion. She got really close to her crotch. I could have sworn her fingers came very close to her sweet spot while Brook and Nancy were gone to the store."

"You know this group? Nothing is sacred. They live a very fast lifestyle. What do you expect? I think they get bored with the same old partner. Fun to get the attention I guess. They all seem to remain friends even after they steal the other person's girl. Got to wonder," Katie commented

"Thank you for your loyalty and love, Katie. You are the best lover and friend."

"As are you, my love. But we'll have to find time for us later because I think I hear the doorbell ringing. It must be the musicians. Will you please let them in?" Katie asked.

"Okay, I am on it. Come in, ladies," Kim invited the new arrivals.

Strange to see female mariachis. Beth can find whatever you need for a great party. Kim greeted the women at the door and took a moment to admire their attire. The women were dressed in beautifully colorful traditional Mexican dresses. Each one had her black hair pulled back with ribbons.

"Come with me and I'll show you where to set up. I'm Kim, by the way and welcome to The Rainbow." The ladies reminded Kim of the women she and Katie had met in Mexico. The leader of the group was Teresa Maria Gonzales. She called herself Tee for short. Stunning and tall, she played flamingo guitar. *I can hardly wait to hear her play.* "I'll leave you ladies to get ready. You can start as soon as you finish setting up your equipment."

"Katie, did you see the women musicians? They are so lovely," Kim commented as she returned to her partner.

"Yes, I saw them. Speaking of lovely, have you seen Darla?" Katie replied.

"I have to admit I lost track of her hours ago. I thought she was with you," Kim said.

"No, I haven't seen her. You said she was poolside?" Katie questioned.

"Could you see if you can find her? I could use her help. I hope she hasn't run off with one of the guests."

"I'll find her. Sure she is chatting with someone. I know she wouldn't be reading her book, too many opportunities with this group," Kim assured her lover.

❧ ❧ ❧ ❧

Kim found Darla playing in the pool with the guests. She had managed to get a volleyball game going in the pool. The guests had chosen teams and they were screaming and groping one another as the ball flew back and forth across the net.

If only we had an underwater camera, what shots we could get. This is Darla's favorite game. I remember many a missing bathing suit tops and bottoms floating in the pool.

"Darla, Katie needs your help. Think you can pull yourself away for a while?" Kim called from poolside.

"Sure, I'll just be a minute," Darla called back.

"No longer than a minute, please."

❧❧❧❧

Jesus what's going on? Jill looks like she has seen a ghost.

"Kim," Jill screamed. "Come to my room right now."

Shit what has happened? Is someone dead? The innkeeper had never seen Jill in such a state. Except for the time she had two women show up at the hotel. She forgot to tell one of them not to join her at the party. That was a sight. She managed to have them both for the weekend. Kim walked very slowly into the room expecting to see a body stretched out on the bed. "Jill, what's up?"

"Trish is missing."

"What do you mean? Did she go for a walk or is she with one of the other women?"

"No, she's gone. I just left her for an hour, went to talk to my friends. She was getting dressed. I came back to the room. She was gone. Vanished."

"Did she leave a note?" Kim questioned.

"No, nothing. Her purse and cell phone are all still here. Look, all here, right here," Jill said in rising concern.

"Don't panic she'll show up. Why do you think this

is so strange?" Kim asked.

"Trish has been getting letters from a fan. At first we thought how cute. Then the letters became more sexual and explicit...more violent. We planned to go to the police after this weekend. We didn't want to spoil the party. I think maybe we may have been followed. She may be in the desert, dead," Jill said dramatically.

"You don't have to be so dramatic. She isn't dead," Kim cautioned.

"If I showed you the letters, you'd change your mind. This person is a real nutcase. I'm not sure if they are dangerous or not. Should have gone to the police long ago," Jill said in regret.

"Let's deal with what we have right now. Trish has been gone for about an hour or two. If we report this, the police will not do anything...have to be missing for forty-eight hours," Kim said.

"Even with the letters? Do you think they might act faster?" Jill asked hopefully.

"I can call a good friend. She's a police officer. See if she can do anything," Kim offered.

"Great. Call right now."

"I will call, but I also need to tell Katie what happened."

❧ ❧ ❧ ❧

Katie took one look at her partner's face and knew something was wrong.

"Kim, what's so important? You look like you've seen one of our resident ghosts."

"I didn't see a ghost. Trish is missing," Kim began to explain.

"Missing? What do you mean, *missing*? Gone for a

walk? In one of the other guest's room fucking? What?"

"I mean she's gone. Not at the hotel. Her purse and cell phone are still in the room. She's been gone for over two hours," Kim said as she fought off the panic she had cautioned Jill against.

"Kim, I just don't see why that's so strange. We need to check the other guest rooms. You know this group, in and out with each other." Katie assured her.

"But there's more to it than that. It seems Trish and Jill have been getting really strange letters from a stalking fan. They are bizarre. I read a couple of them. Very sexual, very sick. They thought maybe they had been followed to Palm Springs," Kim explained.

"Why would they think they had been followed?"

"Jill said a car seemed to be right behind them all the way from LA. She tried to lose the car but no luck. She pulled off the freeway for gas and no sooner had she gotten back on the freeway than it was behind them again"

"Why didn't they call 911...get a cop?" Katie asked.

"Just because a car is behind you isn't a crime."

"No, but now we may have a big crime on our hands. Kim, do you realize what this is going to cause? The police...they will be all over the hotel. KMIR6 will have TV trucks all over us. The weekend will be a bust. Not to mention the negative publicity for us. We need to be very sure she is gone before we call anyone. Go look in the guest rooms please. I will help. You start with the twenties I will go to the thirties. Did you tell Darla about this?"

"No she's still in the pool," Kim said.

"Go and get her now. Let her start questioning the poolside guests. See if anyone has seen Trish."

Kim rushed to the pool to get Darla to assist them.

"Darla, I need you to get out of the pool now. I mean right now."

"Hey what's up, Kim? I've never seen you so upset."

"Darla, this is important. We need your help."

"What's wrong, Kim?"

"Trish is missing...she has disappeared...not in her room...no place to be found."

"Did you check the guest rooms? I saw her eyeing one of the really eerie women when she arrived. She was really coming on to her. I haven't seen the other woman all afternoon. I would bet Trish is with her."

"Do you know what room? Who she came with?"

"She checked in with Nicky, the author. They're in Room 21."

"I will go see if Trish is with her. I'll be right back"

I hope to god Trish is inside even if it causes a fight with Jill.

❧❧❧❧

"Hey, Nicky. I hope I am not interrupting anything. Is Trish inside with you?" Kim asked her guest.

"Yes, you are interrupting and no, Trish, that shit ass, is not with us. She wanted to be. I kicked her out an hour ago," Nicky said.

"Did you by any chance see where she headed?" Kim asked.

"I thought she went back to Jill's room. I told her to keep her hands off my girl. No sooner had I turned my back on Trish than she was all over Dana, tongue in her mouth, hands between her legs. I proceeded to pour a vodka tonic between her legs to cool her off. She left our room. I finished what Trish started. Dana was really heated up and ready to go. Guess Trish did me a favor. I never actually saw what direction she headed. I do know she was very horny when she left us. I thought maybe Jill would get lucky again. Why are you chasing Trish around? Jill got you on the hunt?"

"Well, kind of. We seem to have misplaced Trish. I think you might have been the last person to see her."

"Just go check the other guest rooms. I'm telling you she really needed a fix from anyone."

❧❧❧❧

"Kim, we've checked all the rooms. No luck. Have you found her?"

"No, I think the last ones to see Trish were Nicky and Dana. Trish was trying to get it on with Dana, and Nicky threw her out of their room. Nicky didn't notice where Trish went. She did say she was looking for a good time. Katie, do you think we should call the cops?"

"No, not yet. Let me think about this for a while. I want to talk to Jill myself. See if I can make some sense out of this. Jill might not be telling us the whole story. She could very well have known Trish was fucking with Dana and threw her ass out without her purse or cell phone or money. I remember the time she left a woman at a gas station with nothing, not a dime because she didn't like something she said. Remember that story?" Katie asked.

"Yes, I do. It was sick. But she did come back for her."

"She did, an hour later. Someone could have hurt her. Jill didn't seem to care one bit."

❧❧❧❧

"Jill, I need to talk to you."

"Sure, Katie, we need to find Trish...this is serious."

"Is it as serious as the time you dumped that woman at that gas station?"

"Katie, my little love, this is very different. She is really gone on her own. I had nothing to do with this."

"Jill, are you sure? I don't want to call the police, who will call the FBI. This is a missing famous person case. Not to mention you are her girlfriend. That makes two famous people. The TV news will pick this up in a flash."

"Oh good, Katie, publicity. This can help the film," Jill said as she found a silver lining.

"Jill is that all you think about, your film? From what Kim has told me this could be the work of a stalker, right?"

"It is. I know that bastard has taken her. I expect the ransom call very soon."

"Jill, people this sick usually kill. They don't want money," Katie informed her.

"Death! That would be even better. 'Up and coming super star singer kidnapped and killed as famous director lover is grief stricken. What will happen to the almost completed film? Who will take the stars place? How will the producer find the money to reshoot?'" Jill began to salivate at the possibilities.

"Jill, you are sick. Stop making up the final scene. We need to find Trish. I'm going to gather your guests... see if any of them might know something that will help us make a rational decision."

⁂

"Kim and Darla, get everyone out of their rooms. Tell them to meet us poolside in a few minutes. I don't care what they're doing...just get dressed come outside now," Katie instructed as she took over the search.

"Jill, would you please do me a favor and try and act concerned. I don't need your drama right now."

"Sure, Katie, I'll be quiet as a mouse," Jill replied.

"You had better. I don't have the time or patience to handle your sarcasm," Katie reprimanded her.

"Katie. I've never seen this side of you. What a bulldog. You are awesome. Hmm, really attractive when you're stressed," Jill said.

"Jill, stressed isn't the word for how I'm feeling. I don't feel attractive, quite the opposite. I just would like Trish to appear and right now."

"Katie, I hate to disappoint you but she's long gone. I know her and this is not something she would do. Now I, on the other hand, you can't trust me."

"Humor me, please. Let's think positive. One of these women must have noticed something or someone. I hope she told one of them she was taking a long walk to cool off. I heard she was pretty hot," Katie offered.

"Hot! Why, Katie? She wasn't sitting in the sun and she was locked up with me for hours. I left her to take a shower and get dressed."

"Never mind. It was just a figure of speech. I just want to know she is all right so we can go on with tonight's dinner and entertainment."

❧❧❧❧

All the women were gathered around the pool. Some were pretty wasted from too much sun and drinking. Others looked as if they had just gotten out of bed. Hopefully one of them had seen Trish. Even if it meant she had just slept with her. At this point any sighting would be positive. Katie didn't care if she just crawled out from under a rock. She just wanted to see some flesh.

"Hello, ladies. Kim and I are so sorry to interrupt whatever you had planned. We have a bit of a problem and I'm hoping one of you can help us solve it. Seems Trish has gone missing. She left her purse and cell phone behind in her room. Jill hasn't seen her for three hours. I know Nicky and Dana seem to be the last people to have seen her this afternoon. She left their room some time ago. Did anyone else see her after that time?" Katie asked.

Katie surveyed the women's expressions. All she saw was blank looks on everyone's faces, not exactly what she wanted to happen. *Oh God, please let someone speak. I want to hear something from someone really fast or I may just die.*

"Katie," a voice came from across the pool.

"Yes, Sha. Do you know something?"

"I did see Trish talking to a woman near the front gate. I don't think it was one of us. They seemed to be arguing about something. The woman had hold of Trish's arm. It looked like Trish tried to back up and pull away but the woman grabbed hold of her with both hands as if to restrain her. I thought it was someone she knew. I went back into my room. I was very busy and half dressed...no time to get into Trish's stuff. She was always into some kind of confrontation. I never thought it was out of line just her usual MO. Guess I was wrong," Sha informed the group.

"Sha, could you ID the women if you had to?" Katie asked.

"Sure, I think I could, at least right now. She was about six foot tall, very slim, European looking. Black pulled back hair, very short features. Long, everything about her was long. She could have almost been a transsexual."

"Did anyone else see this woman? Think very hard... the pool has been crowded all day," Katie continued.

"I may have seen her earlier today in the liquor store down the street," Dana contributed. I noticed her. She was very tall, very striking, spoke with an accent, Italian or Greek. Dressed in a black short mini skirt. Could almost see her pubic hair between her legs. You know those foreign girls. She was buying Scotch, expensive Scotch. She left the store, drove away in a Porsche Boxer, gray silver color. I almost wanted to invite her to the party...thought she would be some good meat, you know, entertaining."

"Did anyone else see anything? If not I guess we can assume she went with this person. She isn't here at the hotel. The question is was it willingly? Kim, Darla, Jill, and I need to decide what to do next. If any of you remember anything please come and find us. For now let the party begin," Katie said.

"Katie, are you nuts? Let the party begin? Should we not call the cops?" Kim asked.

"Kim, I will not get overly excited until I know Trish did not leave with this babe on her own. Remember Dana said she was hot. Who knows, maybe this woman was willing to satisfy Trish in ways we will never understand."

"For her to go missing for hours the lady in black must be some fuck! Maybe the stalker is good in bed," Kim offered.

"Let's hope Trish is a happy camper, really satisfied moaning and groaning in waves of pleasure. This is my best hope at the moment. I don't want the police involved or the FBI."

"I know. I can't imagine the mess we would have if the police show up. Trish might be in real trouble. She may be dead. Left to rot in the desert or something. You sure we shouldn't be proactive and call the police?" Kim questioned again.

"Not yet. Give it some time. I want to go to a couple of the local bars and see if I can find the mystery lady or Trish perched on some bar stool sipping Martini's gazing longingly into one another's eyes."

"You sure you want to find the stalker? You could get hurt yourself," Kim cautioned.

"Kim, I need to be sure Trish is really in trouble. If I don't find her or the woman in black, I promise we can call the police tomorrow morning. Right now we need to go on with the dinner tonight...do our best to make it a good evening. Let's think positively. I'll go on the hunt about ten tonight when the bars start hopping. If they are out and about, I will find them. Palm Springs is a small town and you can't hide if you hit the bar scene."

"Okay, but I want to go with you or send Darla," Kim said.

"No, you both need to stay and take care of the party. I will be just fine. I'll have my cell phone on and you can check in to make sure I am okay," Katie replied.

"If you don't answer, should I be worried?"

"If I don't answer, you should worry. I'll make a point to call you also. I promise NOT to approach the woman if she's alone, only if Trish is with her," Katie assured her lover.

"Come on, Kim, let's get things ready for the dinner party. I will go tell Jill our plan and to be sure she hasn't heard from Trish."

⁂

"Jill, Kim and I have a plan before we go to the police. I'm going to go to the bars tonight to see if I can find the lady in black with or without Trish. If I find her alone, at least we know she is still in town and can alert the police. If they are together and look in lust, you have lost your girlfriend for the rest of the weekend. I hope it is the latter," Katie said.

"Katie, you need to be very careful. If this woman is the stalker, she is very dangerous. Her letters got to be very specific–sadistic bondage and all. You should read a couple before you take her on. Come to my room and you can read a few letters then decide if you want to do this alone or just call the cops."

❧❧❧❧

"Goddamn, Jill, these letters are down right scary. This person is a sick puppy. If she has Trish, this isn't good. She is probably, from what I am reading, hanging from some beam, naked and bleeding."

"I know. This is why you need to be very careful. No telling what she might do," Jill warned the innkeeper.

"I don't plan on becoming number two. Please get ready for the party because we need to keep things as normal as possible. I don't want the rest of the guests spooked," Katie said.

"I'll do my best to have a good time. Please let me know when you leave. I want to be sure Kim checks on you every half hour," Jill said.

❧❧❧❧

"Kim and Darla, can you handle the party without me?"

"Sure, my love, the two of us can handle the group as long as Beth keeps the food coming along with the margaritas and wine. I know everyone will be anxious to continue the drinking. I noticed everyone has gone to their rooms getting dressed. It's five and the cocktail party starts at six. I have to get out of these clothes and slip into something more appropriate. I need to find my finest dress for the occasion. Will it be the tight black pants with my see through top? High heels, red, I would guess. A girl has so many choices."

"That's great, love. You keep the party going and we can regroup in an hour. You and Darla should go get started first and I will hang with Beth to make sure she is all right. Kim, don't forget about the entertainers. In all the excitement none of us has talked to them in hours."

"Katie, I'll go see if the lovely Mexican ladies are getting ready to play," Kim offered.

"Great, you go right ahead. Please don't take too long. I know you had your eye on Tee. Just get them started. No need to hang and listen. We don't have time," Katie instructed.

"You know how I love my Spanish women. I'll be back before you know I am missing. Oh, sorry, promise not to go missing. One person is enough."

⁂

"Hola, Tee, can you ladies get started?" Kim asked.

"Si, mi amiga, we will pleasure your group with our wonderful songs."

"Gracias, mi bonita senorita. Sorry, my Spanish is awful. Play as long as you would like. We would love you all evening if that is possible."

"Senorita Kim, anything for you. I would be happy to entertain you all night long."

"Thank you, Tee, that's not necessary. Just make our

guests happy."

Kim stayed for a while waiting for the women to start the music. They looked just stunning. The sound of the guitars and harp filled the night. Their voices were as mellow as the soft breezes through the palm trees. Tee was so gorgeous the guests stopped to listen to her in amazement. Consumed by Tee they surrounded the women, tightening the circle, getting closer and closer. The entertainers began to gather the guests swirling their colorful dresses around them until you could not see the musicians, only the guests. Kim had never seen anything like it. She wanted to stay and watch, but she had other more pressing issues to attend to. She knew Katie needed her.

When she found Katie a few minutes later she couldn't wait to share the good news about the entertainment.

"Katie, the entertainment has started and it's great. You can relax because the guests are enjoying the music and the women. Beth can take her time serving dinner."

"Did you tell Beth?" Katie asked.

"Yes, on my way here I saw her. She is fine. Everyone is fine."

"Everyone but us, Kim."

"I know, we still have a missing person. She is really still missing. I really thought she would come strolling back by now. It's getting late. Maybe she's just trying to teach Jill a lesson," Katie suggested hopefully.

"What a lesson...spoil her entire party? I really don't think Trish would be that stupid. It would ruin her in Hollywood. You don't mess with Jill. I've seen her in action. She can be very vindictive. Do you remember last year when the girl she brought had the nerve to insult Jill in front of her friends? She sent her packing, drug her out by her long blonde hair. No sooner had the woman left than Jill had another babe by her side. It was as if she had a stand in already waiting in Palm Springs. Think Trish will be replaced before we figure out where she is?" Katie asked.

"I wouldn't be surprised? I did hear Jill on her cell phone. Sounded like a very cozy conversation. In fact I thought I heard her say that there was a party in Palm Springs and she asked how long it would take for them to get here," Kim filled her in.

"Kim, I don't have time to worry about Jill's antics. I need to get dressed. I want to go to the bars to see if I can find the lady in black. I'll only be a minute... I need to slip into something perfect for the occasion."

"Don't look too good, baby... I want you to come back," Kim said as she drew her in for a brief hug and kiss.

"Don't worry, I will come back. Hopefully with Trish or at least more insight into what's happened to her."

Chapter Three

The Dark Side

Katie, you look quite stunning. Sure you don't want some company?" Kim asked.

"No, I'll be fine. If I find the dark lady, I want to be alone. She might not approach the two of us. If she is a stalker, she will take the bait and talk to me alone."

"You be careful. I know how you can be fearless and righteous. DO NOT go any place with her if you do find her. Stay around people...don't leave the bar. In fact tell one of the owners to keep an eye on you at all times. If this person is a transgender, she will be strong. Those female hormones do not totally replace the testosterone," Kim cautioned. She really didn't like Katie going out alone but they didn't seem to have another choice.

"I will call you, Kim. I would never place myself in harm's way. I will make sure one of the guards walks me to my car. If I do find her, I would not want her to follow me out," Katie replied.

"Good thinking. Please be careful. I'll be worried until you get home. Come give me a big kiss. Let me slide my hands under that top you have on for good luck."

⁂

Katie found the bar full of people. Toucans was very popular with locals and tourists alike...fun place to dance or just hang. They featured really good drag shows on Sundays. Katie made her way through the guys to the bar. She checked the dance floor on her way.

"Damn, I wish I was four feet taller...the men are towering over me. Makes it hard to see," she grumbled to herself. She decided that she should get to the bar and prop herself up on a high stool to gain a better vantage point. So far, she hadn't seen Trish or *any* tall beautiful women. Just men, a sea of them. Finally she reached the bar. *Great, one stool left. I'll take it.* "Bartender, can you pour me a glass of your best wine please?"

"Sure coming right up."

As Katie scanned the room she still didn't see anyone resembling either of the women she was looking for. "How much do I owe you?" she questioned as the bartender placed her wine in front of her.

"Nothing."

"What do you mean nothing?" she asked.

"That woman across the bar paid for your drink," he said as he indicated the general direction of where the woman sat.

"Okay, thanks." Katie looked across the bar. Searching for her admirer. "Shit." In the opposite corner of the bar tucked in the shadows sat a very tall beautiful female figure dressed in black. Katie could hardly see her because she was well hidden.

"She would like to come sit next to you? Should I tell her it's all right?" the bartender asked.

Katie felt her heart sink along with her stomach. *Oh, no, I think I've found her. Or has she found me? Neither is a good thought. I should call Kim just in case I get into trouble. At least she will know what happened.* Katie decided to slip into the restroom and call Kim but first she needed to figure out what to have the bartender tell the woman.

"Yes, tell her to come over. Let her know I will be right back," Katie blurted in a jumbled rush.

The bartender approached the woman as Katie exited to call Kim. She waited impatiently for someone to pick up the phone at the hotel. It seemed like it rang for ten minutes before she heard the voice of her lover.

"Kim, it's Katie."

"Hi, Hon. What's up? Are you all right?

"Yes, but I think I found the woman in black. She just bought me a drink, and wants to come sit and talk. I haven't gotten to that point yet. I just escaped to the bathroom to call you."

"Do you want me to come to the bar? I want to. I would just watch make sure you're okay or I can send Darla," Kim offered.

"No, I don't intend to make this a long conversation. I just want to get some information. See if she's a local. She might tell me where she has her house if she has one in the desert. I'll get her name if I can and whatever details she's willing to give me."

"Katie, please don't leave your drink unattended, not for a minute. Keep an eye on it at all times. You remember the time I was playing in that bar in Studio City, someone popped Vivian and me a Mickey. We were doped up the entire night, could hardly play. She might get you to leave the bar with her..."

"I will be very careful. I won't finish the wine once she sits down," Katie replied.

"That's a good idea. Please call me as soon as you have the chance. If I don't hear from you in a half hour, I'm coming to the bar."

"Kim, you will hear from me. By the way, how's the dinner going?"

"Just fine. Musicians are still playing. Beth has started the food service. Jill does have another girl. She came right after you left. She appears to be spending the night. Guess Jill is assuming Trish is gone. I thought that seemed very strange."

"Maybe Jill figures they could have a threesome if she showed up? I've got to go. The stalker might think I left the bar," Katie ended the call.

The bar seemed darker as Katie made her way back, her eyes slowly adjusting to the dimmer light. She could see the lady in black sitting next to her empty stool. Katie's wine was right next to the woman's martini glass. Shit! *She had plenty of time to doctor my drink. I might order a martini, wouldn't be too obvious that I wasn't drinking. What will I say to her? Hope she is a good talker.* Katie fretted as she moved across the floor.

"Thank you for the wine." Katie slid onto the stool. The woman was very tall and very attractive. She had a foreign accent, Katie was not sure exactly, maybe Greek.

"You are quite welcome. Do you live in Palm Springs?" the woman asked.

"Yes I do. How about yourself?"

"No, I have a vacation home in Big Horn...lovely golf course. The views are spectacular. I'm on the fourteenth green facing the mountains. The place is small, only five thousand square feet. My house in the Hollywood Hills is much larger, and has a beautiful view. I can see all the way to the ocean on a clear day," the woman offered.

"That sounds wonderful. Do you get to the desert often? I haven't seen you around town."

"No, my job takes me all over the world. I sometimes feel like a gypsy. It's exciting and I see lots of places and have the chance to meet many very interesting people, like yourself. I spotted you from across the bar. I knew we would hookup, maybe share a few moments or more," the woman said as she looked Katie up and down.

"That is very sweet of you. What exactly do you do that takes you away so often?"

"Let's say I'm in the entertainment industry. I search for exotic and different women and men. My company specializes in erotic films. Not porn, I would never film porn. My films are special because of the creatures I cast. I call my actors creatures. They are exquisite when I find them. After I train them they become so very erotic and enchanting. The films are in very high demand."

"Can anyone buy your films?" Katie asked?

"No, my dear, you have to be very special. I have a select group of clients. Many of them are overseas. Very high profile people...men and women, gay, straight, bi, transgender, Royalty and politicians. The business is very profitable. I have many active distributors all around the world. Interested?"

"I don't even know your name. I know nothing about you. Why would I be interested?" Katie asked.

"My sweet pea, I am so sorry. My name is Tasha Palo Marquez Delmonte. What is your name?"

"Katie."

"Just Katie?"

"For now," Katie responded. "Tasha. Should I call you Tasha?"

"My good friends call me Taz, for short. Not sure if we are good friends yet?"

"Tasha, speaking of friends, do you have any in Palm Springs?" Katie asked.

"Yes, a few but they travel quite a bit also. I don't see them much. I do bring many of my creatures with me... we so enjoy meeting new people. Katie, can I interest you in joining us tonight? We can have such a wonderful time together."

"Hmm...I just met you and I'm not the one-night stand type. Plus I do not go home with strangers," Katie turned her down.

"Too bad...you don't know what you're missing. I can guarantee an experience you would never forget. Besides Big Horn is a wonderful place to hang. We really would treat you like royalty," Tasha said as she let her eyes roam over the other woman yet again. "I am so very attracted to you. All I want to do is touch you. Please let me. Your skin is so soft," she said in a husky desire-filled voice. "You are an exquisite creature...so engaging. I can't control my desire to have you right now. Please come with us. Let us please you in ways you have never known."

Katie was shocked at the other woman's attempt at seduction and knew she needed to discourage her and fast. "Tasha it has been nice talking to you but we are not in the same place. I'm sure you'll find what you're looking for but it isn't me. You're very attractive and the right woman will come along but right now I need to get home. It's getting late," Katie said as she began preparations to leave the bar.

Tasha was not going to take no for an answer. She pulled Katie to her. Katie could feel her body against her own. Tasha's breathing became fast as she fondled Katie's back. Her face pressing hard against Katie's was unlike any woman she had ever experienced. Katie started to push her away when suddenly an arm wedged its way between them, pushing the woman away.

"Katie, my love, couldn't you wait for me? I thought we had a date. Seems like you had something else in mind."

Katie breathed a sigh of relief as she realized Kim had sent Darla to be sure she was okay.

"Darla, no of course not, this is Tasha. Tasha this is

Darla. We have a date for dinner tonight."

"Nice to meet you, Darla. You are a lucky women. I was about to seduce your date and have my way with her right here on the bar. She is a fine looking woman. Can I offer you something in exchange? I can give you whatever you desire. You just name it. Money? A trip around the world?" Tasha bargained.

"Tasha, thanks but no thanks. I know how wonderful she is. Why don't we just call it an evening? Katie and I are meeting our friends and they are expecting us."

"Katie, here's my card. If you ever change your mind, just call. I can be reached any where in the world. I will send for you. It would be the trip of a lifetime."

"Thanks, Tasha, I will keep you in mind. Darla and I really have to go. Have a good evening."

The two women were just out of earshot when Katie turned to her rescuer. "Thank God you came when you did. I think she would have carried me from the bar. She is really a sicko. I know now we need to call the cops. If Trish is still alive we will be very lucky. This woman is capable of anything. Her idea of sex and fun is really sadistic. I suggest we find Jill and call off the event for tomorrow night. After this I'm not in the mood to remain happy and calm."

"You're damn lucky I came to get you and not Kim. She would have killed the woman. If she saw the position you were in with the bitch, it would have been all over. I think we need to keep this between us," Darla said.

"You're right. Kim doesn't need to know all the details. If you hadn't shown up, I would be in the Big Horn house with her creatures. I hope Trish is still alive. I bet she's probably drugged. This woman is the stalker. I know she is. I just hope she hasn't got her eye on me. The owners of the bar and the bartenders know who we are and that we own The Rainbow Inn. I can see her showing up again. She did come get Trish at the front door of the hotel. She knows the place. Now she knows who we are." Katie's words were rushed in obvious agitation.

"Do you think she figured out we're looking for Trish? She's smart...she'll catch on fast."

"Darla, at this point I hope she does know. We have her ass. That is why we need to go to the police and not continue the parties. This is getting way out of control. I don't want anyone else hurt. Jill should send everyone home tomorrow."

"Let's hope Jill agrees," Darla said.

"At this point I don't give a rat's ass if Jill ever comes back to the hotel. I have had it this time. Way too much drama for me." Katie declared.

❧❧❧❧

"Thank goodness you two are okay. I was starting to worry. Did you get enough information? Do you think she has Trish?" Kim asked.

"Yes to both questions. She most likely has Trish, and we did get plenty of information. We need to act on it fast. I know she realizes who we are. I want the police involved before she skips town with Trish. Even worse, before she dumps her body in the desert."

"Katie, you're beginning to sound like me."

"For once, Kim, I am sounding like you. I know Trish is in big trouble, maybe dead."

"Darla, go get Jill please. We need to fill her in on what we know."

The moment they were alone, Kim turned to her lover and pulled her into a tight hug. "Honey, I'm so glad you're okay. I was really scared. I sent Darla...I couldn't wait for you to call. I had this sinking feeling in my stomach. I had to do something."

"Sweetheart, you did the right thing. I might have been in Trish's position if Darla had not arrived. This woman is very dangerous. Not to be messed with. She has an unheard of amount of money, not sure how she has amassed her fortune. She said she produces movies, very strange movies. She also has very wealthy clients who buy these movies. I don't have time to go into the details right now, We need to take action. I told Darla we need to tell Jill we're calling off the rest of the weekend. She needs to send everyone home."

Their quiet exchange was interrupted when Jill entered the room.

"Okay, ladies. Darla said you wanted to see me. That you have news. Let's have it. What'd you find out?" Jill demanded.

"Jill, thanks for coming. I just met your stalker. I cannot begin to tell you how scary this person is. She is very sick and I know she's done something awful to Trish. We have to call the police now so they can handle this. I would also like for you to tell your guests, in a very nice way, that they need to go home tomorrow morning. We cannot take the chance of something happening to any more of your friends. This woman has it out for you and anyone associated with you. We don't want anyone else disappearing from our hotel. I know this woman isn't done. She just isn't," Katie told the woman.

"I get the message. I know you're right. If she is the stalker, she does have it out for me. She offered me anything I desired to give her Trish. After I didn't respond you see what happened. She took what she wanted," Jill said.

Darla and Katie exchanged knowing glances. *She*

knows what I'm thinking. Was I next on her list? "She seems to take what she wants. I am calling the police right now," Katie said.

"I'll go tell the guests we're calling off the party and they need to leave tomorrow morning," Jill said.

"Jill, please also tell them NOT to go out tonight and do not answer their doors for anyone. We'll get Maria's brother to come over and stand guard tonight. Kim, will you call and see which brother can come over. I'm off to call the police. Be back in a flash."

"Wait, Katie, I want to go with you," Darla exclaimed.

"Don't be silly. The house is safe. It's locked."

"Darla, why are you being so protective? You never followed Katie around before," Kim questioned.

"Kim, let's say I have good reason to be worried about the both of you right now."

"Darla, I think I'll go catch up with Katie."

"That's a great idea. Just call if you need me."

"Katie, did you get the police?"

"Yes, I did. They're sending an officer right over. I only pray the black dragon is still at the bar."

"We could call the bartender. See if she's still there."

"I don't want to make her suspicious. If she sees him looking at her, she might freak and leave. I know she lives in Big Horn. I'm sure the cops have ways of tracking her down," Katie said.

Chapter Four

The Police

Hello ladies, I am Officer Maria Lopez of the Palm Springs missing persons department. Can you please give me a run down of the events of the last few hours? The dispatcher gave me a brief explanation. You know we usually don't consider a person missing until they have been gone 48 hours. Are you sure she didn't wander off, go to dinner or shopping? Did you check the casino?"

"Officer Lopez, we appreciate your quick response. I'm Katie, one of the hotel's owners. The circumstances surrounding this missing person are very different. We know she didn't wander off on her own. A very dark, larger than life woman abducted her. She was taken from the hotel by force. Two of our guests saw it happen."

"I will need to speak to the guests and get a description and an eye witness account of the abduction."

"Officer, I will be more than happy to have someone find the guests."

"Now...I would like you to tell me exactly what you know."

"All the details?" Katie asked.

"Yes, everything you know. What is the missing person's name?"

"Trish Tobias is her name. She is an actress and singer/song writer. Very attractive blond with deep blue eyes. She is in her late twenties, very thin and tall, maybe five-nine. She has starred in many films and is in the process of making a new movie. The filmmaker Jill Carter is hosting the guests and the party," Katie filled her in.

"I know Jill Carter. I met her at a party in Los Angeles. I was in charge of security for a big bash in the Hollywood Hills. I think at her house. She is some kind of woman. I think I'm beginning to get the picture here," the officer said.

"I'm so happy you understand. I would hate to have to go into detail about this group."

"Katie, you can skip right past who is with whom for now and who is doing who. After that party, I never opted to be her security. Way too much drama. Not quite as bad as what I think we have going on here."

"Ms. Lopez, can I call you *Ms*? Or do you prefer *sergeant*."

"*Officer* will be just fine."

"After Trish was taken from the hotel, Jill told us about a stalker who had been sending letters to both herself and Trish for months. Jill was very worried when the letters became more threatening. Jill planned to call the police in LA when she got home after this weekend."

"Guess she was a little too late calling the authorities," the officer commented.

"Yes, I hate the fact this happened at the hotel. Not good for business having the police called. Not that you aren't a nice person. It's the idea of the cops, the whole uniform thing. Not that I don't like your uniform...I do. It's just the gun."

"Katie, I think you should stop before I have to arrest you for insulting an officer," she said as she hid a smile.

Katie recognized the teasing tone of the officer's

voice and felt more at ease as she continued her tale.

"Jill said she thought they had been followed into town. She then thought it was her imagination. After she and Trish checked into the hotel, they went directly to their room for most of the afternoon. Jill left the room and she thought Trish was was still there getting dressed. Jill got involved with her other guests and Trish went looking for love in all the wrong places behind Jill's back. She had gone into another couple's room and made a pass at one of the women. The woman's partner escorted Trish out of their room. Next thing two of our other guests saw Trish at the front of the hotel with this very tall woman. She was holding Trish by the arms and pulling her towards the front gate. The guests thought Trish had found someone who was willing to have sex with her. They ignored the situation and chalked it up to Trish and her bad behavior," Katie finished briefing the officer.

"Katie, I understand. The party I worked for Jill was about the same. I had a very hard time understanding who was willing and who was being forced to have sex. Looked all the same to me. The good news is no one went missing, at least not for long. Seems this party and the stalker are more serious in their pursuit of sexual favors," the officer said.

"Officer Lopez, what I'm about to tell you is going to make you very mad. Please understand why I did what I am about to tell you."

"This must be good if you already know how I am going to respond. Go ahead try me."

"Kim, Darla and I played detectives. I went to the local bar to try and find the lady in black. I know that sounds awful and dangerous. I will have to agree it was very dumb and very dangerous because I found her," Katie explained.

"Did you go to the bar alone?"

"Yes."

"Did your crazy accomplices let you go alone?"

"Yes, at least for a while," Katie said.

"Going for a second could have gotten you into lots of trouble. I could be looking for two missing women, not just one," Office Lopez said in a lecturing tone.

"I know, not a very smart idea."

"What did you find, madam detective?"

"I found out this woman is very rich, very powerful, and very dangerous. I am not sure what kind of business she's in. All I know is she uses people as slaves for some sort of porno movies. She calls them her creatures, like animals. Seems they do what she wants, willingly, I think. Her lair is in a mansion in Big Horn. The name she gave me was Tasha Palo Marquez Delmonte. Have you ever heard that name?" Katie asked.

"Yes. I know of the family. They originated in Baja, California in the wine country. The family grows grapes at one of the oldest wineries in the Guadalupe Valley. I know them because my family worked in the fields. My father came to the US as a child; his dad is still living in Mexico. The Delmonte winery is still a working, grape producing winery. I would need to ask my grandfather if he knows anything about them. I do know they had many children who left Mexico for other opportunities. I'm sure you're aware Mexico has a lot of drug money and cartels who operate in the valley."

"Kim and I have a condo in Mexico and travel to the wine country very often. We're quite familiar with the culture and the people. We've met some wonderful wine makers and have spent time at their wineries. We've never come across that winery," Katie said.

"I don't find it odd that a member of that family

might be in some kind of strange business. I remember stories as a child. My dad and grandpa would reminisce about the days in the fields. Some of the stories were very scary, murders and killings. Odd rituals took place during the harvesting of the grapes. Wine sometimes being made of human blood. Underground cellars. I know I wasn't going to Valley De Guadalupe any time soon."

"Oh my God. That's amazing. Thanks for the inside information. I know we'll be more careful when we're sipping the red stuff," Katie said.

"Now, please continue with your bar story please."

"Taz, as she calls herself for short, bought me a drink. Then she proceeded to try and seduce me. She wanted me to go with her to her Big Horn house. She became physical, pressing against me, caressing me. She had me in a body lock when Darla arrived, just in time. Darla inched her body between Taz and me. Taz was shocked, not at all amused by the interruption. I could tell she was not used to being interrupted by anyone when on the make. Taz offered Darla whatever she wanted to sell her rights to me to her. I mean she offered her anything in the world. I never thought anyone could become so possessed and desperate. This leads me to the Jill letters. One of her stalker's letters offered Jill anything she wanted in trade for Trish. Jill said she never responded to the stalker."

"Katie, are you sure Jill didn't respond? Are you positive she didn't take Taz up on her offer? This is a great motive."

"Do you really think Jill has something to do with the disappearance of Trish?" Katie questioned.

"Everyone is a suspect, especially the person closest to the victim. The person who has the most to gain. What a perfect alibi, she has the party and all the witnesses."

"You have a good point. I did notice Jill invited

another woman who is here now as if she were waiting in the wings. I did think that was kind of strange."

"I need to question everyone who is here starting with Jill. I have to make a few calls to see if Taz Delmonte is still in the desert, send a surveillance car over to the bar, run a check on her to see if we can get a photo ID. Lots of work to do, besides trying to find Trish, as quickly as possible. I need to call for some help. This is very unusual for our department to run chasing someone before the allowed time. I'm doing this because I know some of the players and suspect foul play. Bear with me...I know you want me to go to the bar and arrest her. I can't. We need more proof other than her trying to seduce a beautiful woman like you. Who wouldn't?" Officer Lopez asked.

"Katie you didn't tell me about the lip lock and the body glove action at the bar. When did you plan on telling me the details?" Kim asked once they were alone.

"Never. It was something I felt you didn't need to know. I knew you would do something stupid like run down to the bar and kill the woman. Then you'd be in jail instead of here," Katie replied.

"You're right...that is exactly how I feel right now. But I will try to rein in my anger."

"Good thinking. We have enough to worry about. I don't think Officer Lopez can question all of the people tonight. She's going to need tomorrow. This means they cannot go home. What a mess. I want all of this to go away. Our beautiful peaceful hotel is now turned into crime central. Look, another cop is coming through the hotel gate. Let's ask Officer Lopez how we should handle tonight and tomorrow. Maybe we can just keep the party going for tonight. I'm sure she'll place someone on patrol overnight."

"You don't think the dark lady would be so dumb

and show up here?" Kim questioned.

"Why not? I don't think she has the brains to care about anything. She is way too rich to get caught. If she did she'd be out on bail and gone to Mexico in a heartbeat. Back to the old country and the wine. From Mexico she could jet off to any place in the world."

"Katie, this situation makes me think of Juliette and the Three Women's Winery. Maybe Taz is one of the three women. You know we have only seen Juliette? We've never met the other two women."

"Kim, don't be silly and overly dramatic. Juliette is a lovely woman. Come on. Remember you promised a trip to Mexico after this weekend. I can hardly wait. I need to get away," Katie said.

"Me too. I want this whole thing to go away. I'm going out to see how Officer Lopez is doing with her questioning. Whatever she is up to I want her to finish fast. I just want to go to bed, wake up and find I was having a very bad dream."

"I'm sorry Kim, but this is real, very real. That woman is very real. Hard to believe people like her exist. She is simply evil, a devil. I would bet she is a member of some cult. Those creatures are probably from the world of the dead or something. Vampires."

"Calm down, Katie, you're beginning to sound like me," Kim said.

"If you had met the woman you would understand what I mean. She was from another world. I was waiting for her to levitate off the barstool. Her hands were ice cold... her lips had a tinge of purple and the eyes, cold as steel... piercing. They were a mirror reflecting my image back to me. I could see the fright in my eyes, scared me even more. I was so happy to see Darla...she saved my life."

"Katie, we need to focus on settling our guests down,

get rid of the police and have everyone leave by tomorrow. Let's go find Jill and Officer Lopez."

❧ ❧ ❧ ❧

"Officer Lopez, we'd like to know how much longer you'll need to question the guests. Will you be finished tonight or at least tomorrow morning?" Kim asked

"Well, ladies, I spoke to Jill. She remembers me from her party in LA. We had a long talk and she has agreed to cooperate with us and has agreed to stop by the station for more questions in the morning on her way home," the officer related.

"That's good. Should make things easier all round," Kim said.

"Yeah, it should. I also talked to the other people you told me had either spoke to or saw Trish prior to Ms. Delmonte allegedly escorting her out of the hotel. They all were very helpful and are also willing to do whatever our department needs to resolve this matter and find Trish. I gathered a lot of information and now I need to put the pieces together," Officer Lopez continued.

"We're very glad our guests are cooperating and you already know that we'll do all we can," Kim assured the officer.

"Yes, I do and I appreciate it. I'm convinced the answer lies in those letters and Ms. Delmonte's connection with Jill, Trish and the other guests. She does have a connection but I'm not sure if she is the stalker or just a very sick individual who enjoys kinky sexual encounters. We don't know if she has Trish or if Trish went home with her. We do know she was the last person we think was with Trish, but I am not sure if that was the case," the officer added.

"It's obvious there's a lot of questions yet to be answered," Katie said.

"Tell me about it. Trish may have left the hotel with her and found herself with the stalker later in the afternoon. We need to get Ms. Delmonte in for questioning. I'll call the precinct and have a car give Ms. Delmonte a visit, see if she is willing to come in for questioning."

"We certainly hope that she gives you the information you need to find Trish and the sooner the better," Kim said.

"This is just the beginning of a long process. Solving this type of disappearance is very slow and hard. The longer the person is missing the less chance we have of finding them alive. That is the sad truth. We have an edge because we have started the search before the required amount of time has passed before a person can be officially declared missing and we begin an actual investigation. She's only been gone for a few hours. And that should work in our favor."

"Officer Lopez, we're counting on that being the case," Kim said.

"I'll be leaving you ladies in a few minutes because I have a lot of work to do tonight. I'll let you know if we have Ms. Delmonte at headquarters tonight. You might sleep more easily if you know we've questioned her and she's still in town. I am leaving an officer on patrol tonight but if you need anything just dial this number and Officer Kline will come running. I would like you to give him a key to the front gate because I want him to do a walk around every couple of hours," Officer Lopez requested.

I'll get you a key," Kim said. "We really appreciate your help."

"By the way can we have everyone check out tomorrow? Do you need them any longer? Katie asked.

"They can all go home, but do make sure you have all their information in case I need to contact any of them."

"Sure I'll do that for you. Anything you need from us we're available until Monday. Heading for our condo in Mexico. Darla knows how to reach us if you need us for anything," Katie replied.

"Great, that would be helpful. I don't think you have to worry about the stalker visiting you. From what I can surmise from all my experience in these types of cases, the stalker, if she has Trish, is long gone with her. She was the target. I'm not sure how Ms. Delmonte plays into this," the officer added.

"We can't help but be worried that she disappeared from our inn and we hope this never happens to one of our guests again so anything you can do to keep our guests—"

"It may just be a coincidence. Trish attracts odd balls from what I've learned from her friends. They were very clear she gets around, travels in a very fast crowd. When you associate with scum you're bound to get yourself in trouble or killed. Drugs and smuggling may be involved. That may be the Mexico connection with Ms. Delmonte," the officer explained.

"Drugs? You think this may be drug related?" Katie asked in alarm.

"We will get to the bottom of this pretty quickly, but, yes, Trish may be in hot water with some drug cartel boss. This is not your average missing person's case. I have a good friend in Immigration and Customs Enforcement and he has a great connections with the Mexican authorities who handle cross-border smuggling of drugs and humans. We have been investigating several cases where women have gone missing only to find them in Mexico in a safe house tied to a chair waiting to be sold or ransomed for cash from rich Mexican families," Officer

Lopez informed the women.

"Oh my God! That's horrible," Kim exclaimed.

"The underworld is very dark and disturbing place. Lesbian women are sought after by rich drug lords. They use them in sex movies or sell them to rich dealers who use them for pleasure, then give them to their runners, who eventually kill them. Mexican authorities have found large grave sites with many bodies in them. Missing persons with no names or faces."

"That just makes me sick," Katie said as she shared a disgusted look with her partner.

"It is horrible but it is also a reality. Mexican investigators told us they found nineteen more bodies buried in the backyard of a house in Tijuana, across the border from San Diego, increasing the tally of corpses found there to thirty-three. Federal agents began digging in the yard in the Mission neighborhood, initially finding six dismembered bodies. The remains date back about five years," the officer continued her grizzly tale.

"Why didn't we know about this?" Kim questioned.

"Because we have just started seeing a pattern of missing women. We could not find them in the US They seemed to just vanish. The Mexican attorney general's office did not say how the victims died or who may have buried the bodies. In the initial raid, Mexican authorities found seventy-five kilos or roughly one hundred sixty-five pounds of marijuana in the house. Cartels frequently use safe houses in border cities to store drugs, house gunmen and dispose of dead rivals."

"I know there's a lot of sickos out there but this is not the dark ages!" Katie declared.

"I see a lot of horrible things in my work, ladies, and much of it makes me sick. I believe Trish may have gotten too close to the wrong people not realizing what might happen to her? Please understand why you are off the hook. Just please do not continue to play detective. It's great you two are getting away for a while. Leave the PI job to the professionals," Officer Lopez instructed the women.

"Officer Lopez, trust me, no more playing detective from us. Will you let us know when you find and talk to Ms. Delmonte aka Taz. It would put our minds at ease if we knew what her involvement might be. She knows who we are and has taken a liking to my partner, Katie. She told our manager and friend Darla she would pay her anything if she would allow her to take her home. The same kind of message the stalker wrote in a letter to Jill when she wanted to buy Trish. Coincidence or connected?" She scares us." Kim questioned.

"You have a point. Just be aware of your surroundings. Be careful, make sure you stay out of strange places, watch your backs for a while until I sort this out," the officer said as she prepared to take her leave.

"Sure makes me feel real safe. How about you, Kim?" Katie asked.

"Sure you want to go to Mexico, Katie?" Kim replied.

"Yes. I love my Mexico. Nothing, not even killings and drugs will keep me away. Besides, we stay out of trouble. I am more worried about the crazies who wander the streets in our own back yard. We need to find Jill because it seems the cops are getting ready to leave, " Katie said.

"Goodnight, ladies. Remember to call the police officer on duty or call me directly if you think of anything. I will call you in the morning or later this evening if we find Ms. Delmonte. Please don't worry. You'll be just fine and we will close this case as quickly as possible. Oh, don't be surprised if the press comes. I put out a missing persons blast on our web site and they always pick it up,"

Officer Lopez said.

"Sure all we need is the press. Katie, the gate bell is ringing could it be them already? I'll go get it," Kim said.

When Kim reached the gate she had her assumption verified when KMIR6 reporter Jessica Long stood waiting to be admitted.

"Hello, can we come in? We heard you had a kidnapping at your hotel this afternoon," the television news reporter said.

"Sure, why not, come on in," Kim offered.

"Would you mind it if my camera crew came in with me?"

"No, bring them all in. We have a party going on. Be sure you don't film any of the guests," Kim cautioned.

"Not a problem. We just want to ask you a few questions. Hope we can help find the missing woman," the reporter assured her.

"Katie, this is Jessica from KMIR6 and she wants to ask us about the kidnapping. Is that what we're calling it...a kidnapping?" Kim asked the reporter.

"Yes, that is what the police are calling it. We picked the news up from their web site for missing persons. They referred to it as a kidnapping," the reporter replied.

"Great you know more than we do. Not really sure what we should be saying to you at this point," Kim said.

"You know, ladies, if I can just mention your hotel and your names that would be great for now. I know this is very hard on you both. Right now we just want to get the word out on our TV news, see if anyone has any leads or has seen Trish. We are just here to help. Television has a way of expanding the search for a missing or kidnapped person. I won't take up much of your time. I have most all I need, got it from the police earlier. I want to take a shot of you two at the front gate and I'll be gone in a flash," the reporter explained.

"That's fine. Take your pictures but, again, be sure not to film the guests," Kim cautioned again.

❧ ❧ ❧ ❧

"Jill, what are you doing? You know these people are from the TV station," Katie cautioned her guest.

"Sure, think I can't spot a film crew? Hi, I'm Jill," she introduced herself as she sauntered up to the reporter. "I'm the girlfriend of the missing person. Feel free to ask me anything you'd like. I want to help in any way I can to find my girlfriend. I'm sick to death. Very worried. She's not just my girlfriend she's the main character in my movie. We're in the middle of shooting. I need her back on the set by Monday. If anyone knows where she is or if she is watching your news story...please put me on the broadcast," Jill requested.

"Yes, of course. Hey guys, turn the lights on. I want to interview Jill. I'll ask you a few questions. Feel free not to answer anything that makes you uncomfortable."

And that quickly Jill was in front of the camera being interviewed by the reporter. Kim and Katie stood in the background astounded by Jill's behavior. It was obvious she was using Trish's disappearance to publicize her movie.

"This is Jessica Long reporting from The Rainbow Inn in Palm Springs. This small boutique hotel caters to lesbians. We're here covering a possible kidnapping that happened earlier today. I have with me the two owners of the hotel and Jill Carter. Ms. Carter is a well known movie producer who is currently working on a feature film. The kidnapped woman, Trish Tobias, is her lover and star of her new movie. Ms. Caarter what is the name of your movie?" the reporter asked.

"Thank you, Jessica. The movie is called 'High Angeles' and it's based on a true story of a young girl's involvement in the world of drugs. The main character is a singer/songwriter who finds herself, as many artists do, involved in the world of drug dealers and drug users. The movie is being filmed in Mexico and the United States. It's a thriller and we have a wonderful cast. Trish, my star, is now missing. If whoever kidnapped her is listening, please let her go. I will do anything to see her home in my arms. I love you, Trish. If you're watching please call the police, if you can," Jill said into the camera.

"Ms. Carter, thank you for your candor. If anyone has any information on the whereabouts of Trish Tobias please call the number on your screen. All information is confidential. This is Jessica Long signing off from The Rainbow Inn downtown Palm Springs. Goodnight."

"Jill, I hope this finds Trish safe. The broadcast will be run tonight on the late news and in the morning. If you're still in town tomorrow, please stop by my office. I would be happy to do another interview with you. Maybe we can cover more details about your movie and your relationship with Trish," the reporter offered.

"Love to. I'll see you tomorrow. Thanks, Jessica," Jill said with a smile as she headed back toward her party.

The reporter turned to the owners of the inn once the movie producer was out of sight.

"Goodnight, Katie and Kim. I hope I didn't disturb you too much. That was a great interview, not often someone who might end up as a suspect takes the chance by giving an interview without legal counsel. Strange woman, that Jill," the reporter said.

"You don't know the half of it, Jessica. Thank you for respecting the other guests. It was a pleasure dealing with a nice reporter," Kim said.

"I'll be talking to you two when and if we get any leads. I would love to interview you under better conditions," the reporter said.

Once she was gone it only took a moment for Katie to turn to Kim and shake her head in astonishment.

"Is it just me or did that interview seem to become more about Jill and her movie than Trish?" Katie asked her partner.

"I think we need to end this party now. What was all that about? Jill ate up the reporter. She wanted to be interviewed. She wanted to answer questions about her film. Maybe all this is a sick act and Jill is behind all of it. Just another full-length movie production for her. She lives in a fantasy world all of her own. Nothing is real for her. I will kill her if she has set this all up," Kim said as her anger began to grow.

"Honey, don't worry. If she is behind this, the police will put her sorry ass in jail. The taxpayers would not be pleased to use their dollars in a scam," Katie assured her.

"I think one of us needs to go have a talk with Jill and make sure she and her party are ready to check out early tomorrow morning," Kim said.

"Why don't we both go...you know united front and all?" Katie offered.

"Sounds fine to me. I just want them gone and all this settled," Kim replied.

"I can't believe she wanted to continue with her party with all of this going on. It doesn't make sense to me," Katie said.

"Let's go get this over with," Kim said.

They weren't surprised to find Jill the center of attention. The party was in full swing...music, drinking, dancing. They went straight to her and pulled her aside.

"Jill, please let's call it a night. I know everyone needs their rest and will check out early tomorrow morning, right?" Kim asked.

"Yes, I'll settle with everyone. I want to pay for the entire planned stay...for the caterer, the stripper, any other charges you incurred. I know I can never pay you for the trouble I've caused you. Please accept my sincere apologies. I never expected this to go this far. I mean the people I sometimes get involved with can be mighty crazy. Trish is a handful. I know she hangs with a very shady element. I never should have exposed you two. I knew we had issues when we started to get those letters. I dragged you into this web. If that Lady in Black is involved, she knows you two. I hope she is just a local nutcase," Jill spouted.

"Jill, we both agree with you. I'm hoping she's just a single woman who likes lots of sex. We can deal with her if that is all she's after. The best thing you can do for us right now is end the party, send everyone to bed and ask them to leave early," Katie requested.

"I'll do that right now. I can settle with you in the morning before I leave. I'm stopping by the police station after I check out. Officer Lopez has a few more questions. I may come back on Tuesday just to help with the search for Trish. I want to post signs and put up a reward for leads, also get more coverage on the local television stations. I want the creep who did this caught," Jill assured them.

"Jill, you're welcome to stay with us alone if you come back to help with the investigation. But please don't bring any more people until this mess is solved. We cannot afford any more missing persons. Keep a low profile around the hotel and no more reporters. Meet them elsewhere," Kim instructed.

"Right, I get it. I'll keep you out of this as much as possible."

"No, Jill, out of it altogether, no press, no friends, nothing," Katie said very firmly, backing up her lover.

❧❧❧❧

"Think Jill will listen to us?" Katie asked once they were alone.

"You know Jill, it's all about her and what makes her happy."

"I want to go to Mexico next week, but I'm a little worried about leaving the hotel," Katie said.

"Darla can handle just about anything. Besides we can get back in two hours. We are going. Let's go see if the party is over, check on Beth and the band. No one has spoken to them all evening. They need to settle their bills. Beth must be really mad her food was not the center of attention this year," Kim said.

❧❧❧❧

"Beth I hope you're not angry with us. We had to attend to the police, news people, and Jill," Kim said.

"No, ladies, I just hope this comes to a good end... somewhat scary, this woman or stalker, whoever took Trish. I'm fine. The food was good, and the guests seemed to enjoy the party despite the added activities. The music was wonderful and it kept people dancing and enjoying the evening," Beth assured them.

"Thanks to you, Beth. You did it all. We hardly moved a finger the entire evening," Katie complimented the caterer.

"That's what friends are for. You've given me so many jobs over the years this is the least I could have done for you. I can see how stressed you two are. Going to Mexico next week?" Beth asked.

"Yes, we'll leave after the guests all check out. Unless we hear something from the police that stops our trip. The sergeant is going to tell us what she has found out about the Lady in Black. I'm actually surprised she hasn't called us this evening. Don't know if that is good or bad news? I hate this waiting around. Makes me nervous," Katie said.

"I'll clean up and get out of your hair. Looks like Jill has cleared the party. No one is around. Not even out by the pool. She really can clear a room? She speaks and they hop to," Beth said as she snapped her fingers for emphasis.

"Wish I had such control," Kim said with a smile.

"We should go check on the musicians," Katie said. "Beth thanks again for the wonderful job you did for this party. Kim and I appreciate all you did."

"Again, it was my pleasure. See you next time," Beth said as they walked away to speak to the musicians.

"Teresa, great job. You really worked overtime. The music was wonderful. I'm really sorry we had a bit of a problem that needed attention," Kim said as they reached the leader of the band.

"Mi amiga, I understand. I'm glad you are all right. I heard you had a scare. Your girl encountered a very dark lady this evening. In our country we would believe this lady belongs to the *Santa Muerte* cult. This cult practices a set of rituals offered on behalf of a supernatural personification of death. The personification is female because the Spanish word for death, *muerte,* is feminine and also because this personification is a sort of counterpart to the Virgin of Guadalupe," Teresa explained.

"Ah, now surely that isn't true," Katie challenged.

"To believers, the entity exists within the context of Catholic theology and is comparable to other purely supernatural beings, namely archangels. The cult involves prayers, rituals, and offerings, which are given directly to *Santa Muerte* in expectation of and tailored to the fulfillment of specific requests. The origin of the cult is uncertain. It has only been expanding recently. The cult appears to be closely associated with crime, criminals, and those whose lives are directly affected by crime," the musician assured them.

"Really? That's fascinating but at the same time terrifying," Kim said.

"Criminals seem to identify with *Santa Muerte* and call upon the saint for protection and power, even when committing crimes. They will adorn themselves with her paraphernalia and render her respect that they do not give to other spiritual entities. I have only encountered members of this cult while performing at a party in the wine country, the Guadalupe Valley. The valley is named after Saint Guadalupe. I was very afraid and could not wait for the party to end. Many old wine makers had ties to these cults and the drug lords. Be very careful, mi Amiga. Stay away from these people, they can harm you and your loved ones," Teresa warned them.

"Thank you so much for the information. We will be very careful," Kim said.

"Please see that you do."

"Thank you again for the wonderful entertainment. Everyone loved your music. I'm just so sorry I couldn't enjoy it. Maybe next time. I know Beth knows how to reach you," Kim said.

"Kim, here is my personal card. If you need any music or just want to talk, call me any time. I'm here for you. I'm very knowledgeable in these matters. The Mexican culture is very different from that of the United States. This is a very serious situation. Many of these people have connections all over the world. They work as a group to commit unspeakable crimes to satisfy their own desires," Teresa said.

"Teresa, I cannot tell you how grateful I am that you would give of your time for us. You just met us," Katie added.

"You are wonderful and kind people. I'm sorry you have to go through this. Bad people somehow find the good souls, have a need to capture and control them. They want to consume the good and turn it to evil. I will keep you two in my prayers. God be with you both," the musician said.

❧❧❧❧❧

Kim and Katie found themselves alone in the common area.

"Katie, everyone is in bed. Beth is gone, so is Teresa and her girls. We can close up and go to bed. I'm exhausted. I feel as though I've been up for days," Kim said as she drew her lover in for a hug.

"Me too. I just want to sleep. Tomorrow will bring an end to this madness, I hope," Katie replied as she snuggled into the warm and comforting embrace.

"My dear little Katie...yes some of the madness will end. We still have a missing person and the Lady in Black is still at large. I hate that she knows us. I hate that she is fixed on you," Kim said.

"I am sure she has forgotten me and found another obsession. She was hot to find someone. It did not necessarily have to be me. She wanted to take someone home for a night of fun and games. I know she moved on to the next piece of meat at the bar. All she wanted was a sexual fix with some sadistic activity. I bet she still has her catch in the sack," Katie assured her partner.

"Speaking of the sack, I'm ready for a shower. Want to join me?" Kim asked with a hopeful grin.

"No, I have a few loose ends I need to tie up from the day. I need to check the grounds, make sure all the guests are in bed, turn off the lights, secure the doors. You know the details," Katie replied.

"I'll help you. I forget the details, sorry."

"Go take a shower. I'll be right in. It won't take me long."

"Be very careful and please do not leave the hotel. If you see anyone, come right back into the house," Kim cautioned her lover.

"I will. I won't stop to chat. Be back in a flash," Katie assured her. She stood on tiptoe and gave Kim a loving kiss. "Now go shower."

⁂

It seemed very quiet as Katie made the rounds. The grounds were empty. She heard the sound of an owl in the distance. The sky was dark and the stars bright. Katie felt like she could see for miles through a blanket of tiny specks through to the smallest galaxies. She wanted to sit and relax beneath the soft blanket the desert sky offered. But she knew Kim would worry and think she'd been kidnapped. She avoided the temptation to linger by reminding herself to finish her rounds and get back to the house. Kim didn't need an additional stress. But then she heard something.

What was that?

Katie was certain she had seen a figure from the side of her eye. Just a flash. *Was it the wind through the palm trees or did I see something? I'm heading back to the house.* Under other circumstances she would search the property. As she turned towards the house she felt a hand on her shoulder. She froze in place, afraid to turn and look. *Should I scream? Don't be stupid just turn and look behind you.*

"Katie, sorry I didn't mean to startle you. I just came out for a breath of fresh air."

"Shit, Jill, I thought we agreed everyone would stay in their rooms tonight."

"I know. I just needed to take a walk...thought if I took some time alone I might remember some important facts I could tell the cops tomorrow. My only conclusion after reviewing the past few months with Trish was her involvement with those drug friends. I know they have something to do with the kidnapping. The woman she left with was just some babe she met who fixed on her. She isn't the stalker. I'm gonna turn in for the night. See you in the morning. Night," Jill said as she turned away.

⁂

"Katie, was everything okay?" Kim asked.

"Yes, ran into Jill. She was restless. Needed to regroup and think about Trish I guess. I know somehow she is involved with this. Not directly, but she knows why this has happened."

"Bet you're right, Katie. Jill has some enemies who would love to see her fall, get arrested and put away for kidnapping. I will be glad to see the sunlight."

"Let's get some sleep. I'm exhausted. I'm going to take a shower and will join you in a few," Katie said.

"I'll be asleep before you hit the pillow," Kim complained.

❧❧❧❧

The night was still and quiet. Katie and Kim slept with one eye open. Neither wanted to speak. They lay in silence, reviewing the events of the day over and over again. Dawn came slowly. The way it does when you're awake and want it to be morning. The sun rose at six-thirty. Birds chirping. All was well with the world. Kim rolled over to look at Katie. Her eyes were wide open, staring back. Kim softly kissed her on the cheek. They both smiled, still tired, knowing they had to face another day, hoping the group would all leave bright and early.

"I'll make the coffee and you stay in bed for a while."

"Thanks, hon. I just want to lie here a few more minutes. Need to get my head together. This morning will not be easy. I'll get the paper when I get moving."

❧❧❧❧

They both moved very slowly, sipping their coffee, watching the AM show trying to read the paper.

"Shit, Kim look at the headlines: *Lesbian Hotel Kidnapping.*"

"Read it to me," Kim requested.

"The Rainbow Inn, a quaint inn that caters to lesbians, reported a kidnapping yesterday afternoon. One of the guests was abducted from the inn's grounds around 3 p.m. Witnesses said they saw the guest leave under force with a very tall woman dressed in black," Katie read from the newspaper.

"Oh damn! This is all we need. People will be afraid

to stay here," Kim complained.

"Do you want me to read this to you or not?" Katie asked.

"I'm sorry, baby. Please go on."

"The missing woman was part of a party hosted by Jill Carter, a prominent Hollywood producer. The missing woman is Ms. Carter's girlfriend and star of her up-and-coming movie, which is still in production," Katie continued to read.

"I can't help but wonder if this is somehow a publicity stunt for the movie." At the look from her lover, Kim went silent.

"Ms. Carter seems very upset and would like anyone who might know the whereabouts of Trish Tobias to please call the Palm Springs Police Department. Ms. Tobias resides in Beverly Hills, California. She was last seen leaving The Rainbow Inn in Palm Springs. The owners of The Rainbow Inn, Kim Ferraro and Katie Richardson, along with their manager Darla Clark, expressed deep concern over the kidnapping. They said nothing like this has ever happened in the 15 years the inn has been in business. They send their thoughts to Trish's family and friends and hope she is found very soon. Anyone with information is urged to contact the Palm Springs Police Department," Katie concluded.

"Katie, our phones should be ringing off the hook. Our guests will be calling, so will the friends. I want to leave today for Mexico and let Darla handle the calls. She is so good with situations like this."

"When has this ever happened?" Katie asked.

"I didn't mean exactly like this. We have had some very strange events over the years. Remember the two women who woke Darla up at four in the morning, got her out of bed because they thought they heard people walking on the roof of the hotel?"

"Yeah, I remember them When she got to their room, not only were there people on the roof but in the trees and inside the room, according to them. They thought they saw wires in the trees with listening devices. Poor Darla had to follow them all over the property as they pointed at what they thought were wires and people darting around on the rooftops," Katie recalled. The women shared a laugh that helped break the tension of the last several hours.

"Darla, bless her heart, listened to them and then called the police. They came to her rescue. The very nice police officers made sure the hotel was secure and reassured Darla the women were on something and paranoid, not harmful. They did not arrest them, which I thought was strange. Darla spent the entire night painting the room next door to the women's room, even though the room did not need painting. She happily escorted them out of the hotel by six a.m," Kim added.

"Guess you're right. She has handled a few unfortunate situations. Thank goodness, nothing like this one," Katie said.

"Officer Lopez was going to stop by this morning with information. I'm shocked she didn't call last night. That must mean she was unable to find Taz, also known as Ms. Delmonte. We need to hang around until she gets here. We also cannot leave Darla here to check out Jill's crowd alone," Katie said.

"I know. We have things to do, cannot escape the madness. I am going to call Lopez and see if I can get her ASAP," Kim said.

"While you're calling Lopez, I'll get the troops moving on out. Good thing Jill has paid for everyone. We don't have to spend time chatting with everyone. Maybe they've all left. I'll go check."

⁂

The hotel looked beautiful. The sun was shining, birds singing, and the mountains were green with spring flowers. One would never know what happened there just the day before. All of the guests had checked out. Most likely they could hardly wait to leave. Katie knew she'd feel the same way except for the fact she was the boss. *Here comes Jill. Looks like she's the only one left.* "Hey, Jill, I see you cleared everyone out early."

"Yes, Katie, they all wanted to leave before that Lopez woman arrived. You know my girls they don't like trouble. I sent my new friend packing very early this morning. I didn't want to give Officer Lopez the wrong idea. I think she already dislikes me. We have a bit of history, that cop and me."

"I'm sure you have nothing to worry about, Jill. Officer Lopez is just doing her job."

"I would guess she thinks I have something to do with Trish's disappearance. You know the partner is always the first suspect. Hateful, all of this. I should have followed my instincts and called the police weeks ago. No, I was too busy, blew it off, said that I can take care of this later. Wrong," Jill said.

"Hindsight is always much clearer. I just hope the police figure this all out," Katie replied in a consoling tone.

"Well, I believe we're all settled. I'll pack and get on my way. I need to stop by and see Officer Lopez on my way out of town. I'm sure she has more questions."

"Yes, she said she was expecting you to stop by," Katie said.

"Tell Kim and Darla goodbye. I hope I haven't

caused you too much stress. If I can pay you for this, please tell me how much. I feel so bad. I never would want you guys to be hurt in any way. I hope that woman in black is far away," Jill offered.

"Jill, you're a valuable guest and I feel certain there was nothing you could have done to prevent this so don't give it another thought," Katie assured her.

"Please call me if anything happens. I know we need to stay in touch. I imagine Lopez will want me back here soon. I want to come back, see if I can find Trish."

"We'll let you know if we learn anything and you do the same," Katie said.

"In my heart, I know she is not in the desert. I think she is very far away from here. I wish I had the luxury of searching for her, but I still have to deal with the movie," Jill said.

"What will you do about the movie?" Katie asked?

"We need to continue to shoot or stop, which costs our investors big bucks. I do have interruption insurance and a big policy on Trish. This will add to a motive for my being involved in her disappearance. Oh, God help me please. If I find Trish and she is on a fling, I will kill her myself."

"Jill, just go do what you have to do. Don't worry about the police. Keep your senses and find help...get a lawyer right away," Katie suggested.

"I will. I have a few on staff. Love you, Katie, see you soon."

Jill and Katie hadn't much more than parted when Kim came rushing in. "Katie, I got hold of Lopez and she's coming over now. She wanted us to tell Jill to wait for her. Seems like she has some very interesting things to tell all of us. I'll find Jill and tell her to stay around."

"Jill was just here saying goodbye. She shouldn't be

too difficult to find. She said she was going to go pack. We can meet in the house and I'll make some coffee. I'm sure we could all use the caffeine after last night."

❧ ❧ ❧ ❧

"You got here fast, Officer Lopez. Come in. Like some coffee?" Katie invited.

"Love some, thanks. I take it black," Officer Lopez requested.

"Why did I know that?" Katie asked with a laugh.

"Kim and Jill will be here any second. Make yourself at home."

"Nice place you two have. Sweet setup, hotel and lovely home. You must love what you do."

"We do love our business and our guests. It's fun but lots of work twenty-four/seven. We do escape to the condo in Mexico though when we can," Katie offered.

"Yes, we talked about Mexico. I have some very interesting information, and Mexico enters into it. I'll wait for the others before I give you the details," the officer said.

They didn't have long to wait before they were joined by the other two women.

"Officer Lopez. I hope you have good news for us," Kim said.

"Good morning, ladies. This won't take long. I know you have work to do. Glad I caught you, Jill. Saves you a trip to the station. Sit down. I have some news about Trish and the woman of interest, Taz."

"Is she okay? Did you find her?" Jill questioned hopefully.

"We were unable to locate Ms. Delmonte last night. Our officers went to her house and it was closed up. Papers in the driveway. Looked as if no one had been in the house for weeks. We questioned the neighbors. They said they had seen a Porsche parked in the driveway earlier that evening and someone had been in the house but left that evening and never returned," Officer Lopez explained.

"Does that mean they've fled the area?" Jill asked.

"I asked if they had noticed if the car or anyone had been in the house other than yesterday. They told our officers a few strange cars came to the house... people went in and out carrying boxes and crates and it looked like they were moving. The Porsche was at the house alone. The other cars had gone earlier before the Porsche arrived. So, yes, it does look like they've cleared out," Officer Lopez said.

"Tell us more, Officer Lopez. Do you know where they went?" Katie asked.

"We asked if they saw the driver or anyone with the driver. They hadn't seen anything, just the people with the boxes. We went to the bar and spoke to the bartender who said Ms. Delmonte had arrived at the bar right about the time you arrived and that you had been the only person she spoke to that evening. She left right after you and Darla. The bartender did say he had seen Ms. Delmonte in the bar the night before with a woman who had come in with her. He said they seemed very cozy and they were kissing and having sex at the table. We asked for a description and he said she was blonde, tall, very attractive and not at all shy," Officer Lopez said.

"Hmm…that could've been Trish," Jill said.

"They danced with many of the other patrons during the course of the evening. The tall, dark haired women seemed to take pleasure from watching the blonde seduce the men or women, whoever she was dancing with. At one point both women had a very nice looking girl sandwiched between them. They both undressed her and fondled her, kissing her breasts and pressing their hands between their bodies in an obvious fucking motion."

"Oh my God! Katie, you were with that woman. I'm so glad you escaped her unharmed," Kim exclaimed.

"Go on officer," Jill requested.

"The bartender had to call the bouncer to stop the action before someone called the police. The three of them left shortly after. As they left they could hardly stop feeling one another. The bartender said it was very erotic. They must have gone back to the house that night."

"Are you saying that you have no idea where they are?" Jill asked.

"There are a lot of unanswered questions, Jill. What made Ms. Delmonte come to the hotel for Trish the next day? How did she know Trish? Why did she then go to the bar that night alone and try and pick up Katie? What happened to the other two women she was fucking, and was the first one Trish? Excuse my language, sorry."

"Yes, that's a lot of questions, officer," Jill agreed.

"My fear is that the crates the neighbors saw being carried from the house were the size of coffins, large enough to hold a body from the description given to us. The witnesses couldn't remember how many boxes came from the house. They stopped watching after a while. If, let's say, the crates did contain bodies dead or alive, was Ms. Delmonte seeking yet another victim at the club that night?"

Once again Kim looked at her partner with a horrified expression on her face. She reached out and took Katie's hand, bringing it to her lips for a gentle kiss.

"These questions will go unanswered until we can locate Ms. Delmonte and bring her in for questioning. We have an APB out on her and her car. My guess is that she is in Mexico by now. Her family would protect her at all costs. She knows we suspect her," Officer Lopez said.

"Do you think there's any chance you'll find her?" Kim asked.

"All I can promise you is that we'll do our best since we believe she headed south of the border. It will not be hard to find her but it will be hard to convince the Mexican police to turn her over to us for questioning. She is from a very prominent family in the wine country. They have lots of power with the authorities and have connections with the drug cartels," the officer said.

"Surely that won't allow them to get away with kidnapping Trish," Jill asserted.

"This is a very hard case. We have had missing women who turn up, sometimes dead and sometimes alive, who had been taken and sold into sex slave rings in Mexico. Ms. Delmonte may be involved with this ring. If she is, I can assure you this case will remain open for a very long time, with no resolution," Officer Lopez said.

With every word the officer spoke Kim and Katie's hearts sank a little lower.

"There has to be some way to find Trish and free her," Kim said hopefully.

"All we can do is narrow the suspects down, ask for the public's assistance and hope for a break in the case. Sorry for the bad news," Officer Lopez added as she got to her feet.

"Officer Lopez, you will do your best for Trish won't you?" Jill questioned with the first genuine concern she'd shown.

"Of course I'll do my best. That is my job after all. Jill, you can go back to town. I will call if I need you to answer more questions and I will in a few days, so hang around please. I don't need you and Katie for anything. You have told us all we need to know. If you encounter anyone or hear anything we should know, you have my numbers. Just please do not play detective. You can get hurt. I'll be leaving, got lots of work to do and the longer we wait the less likely it will be we will find Trish. Thanks for all of your help," the officer said.

❧ ❧ ❧ ❧

"Goodbye, Jill, have a safe trip home. Katie and I will be heading for Mexico later today for some R and R."

"You guys stay out of trouble. Remember what Officer Lopez said about Ms. Delmonte and her family in Mexico and the sex rings down there," Jill cautioned.

"We'll stay away from her and her family, believe me. She would have to know a lot about us to find us in Mexico. Right, Katie?"

"Let's not worry about Taz. She is not coming after us. I want to go relax, drink some good wine and walk on the beach. Come on. I need to get Darla moving and Maria cleaning the rooms. They both have lots of work to do. We are full again next weekend. Once I get them going we can leave. Why don't you go and get ready. Pack up the car and take some food. We have nothing at the condo. I'll join you shortly," Katie said.

Chapter Five

A Mexican Moment

Kim was glad she and Katie could finally get away to their Mexican hideaway. They bought a beachfront condo along what is now called the Gold Coast of northern Baja, which stretched from Tijuana to Ensenada. Yes, the ugly Americans are moving to Mexico. Baby boomers who find it hard to retire in the US, have found Mexico. Donald Trump is building a grand four-tower mega spa resort complex just north of their condo complex. He, along with many other developers, were flooding the beach front property with mega high rises.

They had noticed the influx of gay men strolling along their beach walking around downtown Rosarita, shopping, eating, and cruising the young Mexican boys. Mexican young men are very pretty with very little hair on their slim young bodies, such a treat for the aging gay male. The town was changing to an art colony circa Laguna Beach in the early 1930s and where art goes so do the gay men. Not to mention the real estate values.

When a gay guy buys a house, it becomes a decorator's palace. Those gay boys sure know how to prissy up a place. History proves that where the gay men come, the lesbians are soon to follow towing their U-Hauls with the new girlfriend. Me casa su casa.

Mexico has lots to offer. Low cost beach front houses with very low property taxes, fifty dollars a year, one hundred dollars tops. If you like fish, this is the place. Fresh caught fish, lobster, shrimp, really inexpensive meals. Margaritas and beer flow freely in the restaurants. Entertainment is year round. Singing, dancing, mariachi bands. You can find a fiesta on a Sunday afternoon any place you visit.

Katie and Kim's all time favorite place to spend a Saturday or Sunday afternoon was in the wine country. The Guadalupe Valley Wine Country in Mexico is a short hour's drive south along the Big Sur coastline of Northern Baja. The roads are better than Highway 1 along the northern coast. The wide-open expansive views off the cliffs across the ocean were breathtaking.

When you approach Ensenada's port, you can see the cruise ships docked with thousands of tourists drinking tequila, eating chips and salsa, and dancing to the beat of pounding disco music from the seventies. For some reason the Mexicans seem to think Americans enjoy those songs. From the looks of the ship's passengers, they have no problem shaking their booties to the beat.

Kim and Katie were not in the mood to party with them. They headed straight for the Vino Cota. Winding along a two-lane road for about half an hour to the first winery off a long dirt road. They bumped along to a winery owned by a very beautiful French woman. She moved to Mexico to follow her dream of making Mexican wines. Juliette is her name. A striking tall, thin woman with a longing gaze and wonderful French accent, her voice was like a fine red wine as it passed her large, red lips. She always had a group of friends sitting around a very large Mexican carved, wooden table in her lush gardens. They were sipping wine and engaging in what seemed to be fun conversations when the women arrived.

Kim's gaydar immediately pinged identifying

Juliette as a lesbian. It was obvious all the women around her garden table were lesbians. Katie read her partner's thoughts easily."You think everyone is gay," she said.

"Lesbian or not, they all should be lesbians," Kim replied.

This unique artisan winery was named Three Women Winery, a bit of a challenge to find, but well worth the effort. Three women, Juliette Gaillard included, teamed up in a cooperative manner to create three interesting and unique styles of wine making. These wine artisans pooled their energy, talent, and vision into perfecting the art of handmade wines. This communal effort had built a dedicated family of friends and visitors who seemed to embrace the idea of cooperation can achieve anything.

Quite often visitors and wine tasters who visited the winery were touched by the spirit of it all and found themselves jumping into action. Total strangers who happened along have been known to help with harvesting, bottling, moving barrels, cracking walnuts, gathering fresh eggs, or whatever else seemed to be happening at the time. Three Women and their friends were a prime example of people working together in harmony, having fun, while improving the quality of life for all involved.

During their visits over the years Katie and Kim had learned a lot about Juliette Gaillard. She was a skilled and talented ceramic tile artist in addition to being a wine maker. She created individual tiles and designs and unique custom tile work for stairways, walls, bathrooms, murals, walkways and more. Her ceramic tile work could be found in galleries and in homes from Ensenada to San Diego.

She began her courses on ceramics in 1985 at the University of California San Diego, studying with French artist Irene de Waterville, and continuing art classes at the Rhode Island School of Design. Hand-painted tiles had been her major interest since 1989 allowing her to develop a variety of designs from Mediterranean, surrealistic and medieval. More recently she had focused on the flora and fauna of Mexico's premier wine producing region of Guadalupe Valley. Katie and Kim loved to visit the winery. With each visit they experienced more than expected.

They parked the car next to a ranch wood fence. Once they were out of the car, they petted the golden retriever lying next to the fence. He appeared to be the guard dog. They approached the door to the beautiful wine cave where Juliette aged all her wines. At first it was dark as their eyes grew accustomed to the candle light that illuminated the stored bottles of the elixir of the Gods, Juliette's fine wine. Their eyes quickly became accustomed to the cave's lighting. They saw Juliette approaching the door to the cave. Her slender figure seemed like an apparition as the sunlight mixed with the cave's lighting, making her appear as a mystical creature.

She greeted them with warmth and pleasure, "Hola mi amigas. Buenos tardes. Como esta?"

"Bien Bien e tu?" That was as far as Katie and Kim's Spanish went.

Juliette in her shy seductive way was doing the Mexican thing making them feel at home.

"We came to taste your new wines. What are you serving today?" Kim questioned.

"For mi amigas we will taste the finest of my new vintage. I have a bottle of tinto (red), a mixture of cabernet sauvignon, merlot and cabernet franc grapes, hand picked by mi amigas, from some of the oldest and most venerated vineyards in Mexico. We hand sort before crushing in the traditional manner. We have aged this wine for twenty months in one hundred percent new barrels, of French oak from my home country."

Kim's lips were parched and she ran her tongue over them trying to moisten them. She couldn't wait to taste the succulent blend. Juliette opened one of her bottles and placed it on an oak barrel using it as a serving table. She added three glasses next to the bottle where it shimmered from light provided by the candles.

Juliette poured just a taste of the red blend into the glasses. She swirled the liquid in a pulsating spin... it almost could make you dizzy as the candle light danced to the rhythm of the spinning wine. Finally, Juliette handed Katie and Kim their glasses, the foreplay almost too good to end.

They sipped the wine. It was smooth and rich, making the women thirst for more. Sensing their need Juliette poured each of them a second glass, this one full. As they sipped the wine, the room seemed to fill with an extraordinary light as if the candles' light now blazed with the wine-maker's passion. Her eyes glowed with heat, her hair now hung freely billowing across her bare shoulders. Katie seemed to glow in the light and they both appeared to take on a hot steamy look as if they could explode and disappear before Kim's eyes. It must be the wine.

Suddenly what seemed to be another figure stood at the entrance of the cave. Juliette motioned to the woman to enter the cave. It was one of the women Katie and Kim saw sitting at the picnic table. Tall and almost handsome, she walked towards them. Juliette poured the beauty a glass of wine. She also refilled the women's half-empty glasses.

Juliette introduced the young beauty as Sera. She was one of Juliette's helpers. Kim's mind began to wander under the influence of the wine. Her thoughts posed many images of exactly what kind of helper Sera might be. Suddenly it became clear what Sera was to Juliette as the women began to move closer to one another, Sera's hands caressing Juliette, pulling her beautiful hair away from her shoulders, exposing an almost bare chest.

Cloudy from the wine, Katie and Kim backed their bodies against the cave wall out of the glow of the candle light. The two women continued their show, the passion obvious to the onlookers. The cave became a sauna as the heat from their bodies filled it with a steam that one could not help but breathe in.

Katie and Kim, transfixed, could not take their eyes off of them. They groped every inch of each other until it was obvious they would complete the ritual. Juliette shocked her guests when she pulled away from her lover as if to invite them to join in their passion. Their hesitation let Juliette know they had not had enough of her poison to partake in the enjoyment the women were experiencing.

Suddenly Juliette pressed her wet body against Katie's. She reached over, lifted the wine bottle above Katie's breast and began to drip the wine between her exposed breasts. Then she licked the deep red liquid as if she were sipping and sucking it into her mouth, using her lips to caress every last drop of the juice.

In shock and disbelief Kim stood motionless against the cave wall. Suddenly a hand slipped between her legs. Sera slowly moved her toward Katie and Juliette. The four began to press and move against one another. The room began to spin, the candles flickered in rhythm with the four bodies. Katie and Kim felt drugged. The wine had taken over their senses, overcoming all their inhibitions.

Is this really happening? I must be dreaming? Katie and I would never do this. Suddenly Kim found herself propped up on a wine barrel in the corner of the cellar slumped over leaning on the dirt wall. As her eyes opened, she could see Juliette, Sera, and Katie through the dimly lit room drinking and laughing.

⚜ ⚜ ⚜ ⚜

"Hey, Kim, have you been taking a nap?" Katie asked.

"Have I been sleeping? How long?" Kim replied.

"I don't know, Kim, we've been having such a good time that I lost track of time. I do know it's dark. We cannot drive home to the condo at this hour. What do you suggest we do?" Katie asked.

Juliette graciously offered them a place to spend the night.

"Katie, I can drive," Kim insisted.

"Sure, Kim, you have been passed out from too much vino and you want to drive. I'm not going to end up in a Mexican jail. You can if you want to go home alone."

I guess my dreams left me a little scared to stay with Sera and Juliette. If in fact it was all a dream? I am not so sure, Kim thought.

They followed Juliette out of the cave and down a long path to a small casita behind the main house. Juliette opened the door. It was lit with candles similar to the wine cave. In the corner was a kiva fireplace. It was burning as if it was already welcoming guests.

Did Juliette know we were spending the night? Kim wondered.

"Katie, we have nothing to sleep in," Kim warned.

Juliette opened up a beautiful Mexican dresser pulled out two very lovely silk nightshirts and tossed them with a swift movement almost inviting the women to disrobe.

"Thank you so much for your hospitality. We hope we are not inconveniencing you," Katie thanked their hostess.

"No, my lovely ladies, you are so very welcome. I will leave you to freshen up. You will find everything you might need in the bathroom," Juliette said as she took her leave.

"Shit, Katie, this place is all set up for guests. How convenient, don't you think?"

"You have such an imagination. Just relax for once. Look, Kim, on the table fruit, Mexican cheese and, of course, one of Juliette's fabulous wines."

"Haven't you had enough wine for today?" Kim asked.

"After the last few days, I can never drink enough good wine. Here, I'll pour you a glass, after all, you have been snoozing for a few hours," Katie accused.

"Katie, what did you say? A few hours?"

"Yes, my love, look at your watch. It's seven in the evening and we got to the winery at two this afternoon."

"No way did I sleep that long. What did you and the girls do while I was out?" Kim questioned with suspicion.

"We chatted, and Sera and Juliette took me to a very private vault where the women stomp and prepare the grapes for the barrels. It was just like I had stepped into a dream. I thought I was in another world. I will have Juliette take you on a tour tomorrow or maybe later tonight if you are up for more wine. Let's get freshened up. I believe Juliette and Sera will be serving us dinner."

"You think this Inn serves dinner *and* good wine?" Kim questioned.

"Well, of course, my love."

Katie and Kim slipped into the shower, tiled with traditional Mexican stone inlaid with striking blue accents with glass chips in the shape of grapes and vines. This was, of course, Juliette's handiwork. The water almost tasted as if it had been spiked with sweet grape essence. The light above the shower was tinted purple, which gave the water the look of dark red wine.

As they stood holding one another they sipped the water as it rained over their faces and trickled over their naked bodies. The bars of soap were in the shape of a bunch of grapes, small and tightly clumped together. The fragrance filled the shower with the sweet smell of raw pleasure. They caressed one another as they bathed with the soap and water. The pleasure filled their souls. They felt enchanted and relaxed.

"Katie, I love you very much. You're very beautiful. Thank you for your love and kindness."

"I love you too, Kim."

A knock on the door followed by Juliette calling them interrupted their gentle loving.

"My lovely ladies, dinner will be served in the main house in a half hour. When you are done come join us. You will find clean clothes in the dresser. Please help yourselves," Juliette called to her guests.

"Damn, we have to get out of the shower. Let me wash your back."

"Okay, but that's all. It would be rude to be late for dinner."

❧❧❧❧

"Katie, look at this," Kim said in awe.

"What?"

"The clothes."

"What about them?" Katie asked.

"They are exquisite. I've never seen anything so sensuous and flowing," Kim said as she pulled the shirt over her head.

It clung to her body like a part of her own skin. Her tight aroused nipples were visible where the soft fabric hung like streams over them. The blue jeans clung to her hips and butt as if they had been poured onto her body. It was strange she couldn't feel the constraints of them. She felt naked.

"God, Kim, you look like a dream. Come over here so I can pinch you. I want to make sure you're real." Katie said.

"I know. I don't feel real. I haven't felt real all day. This whole experience seems like a dream. What else is in that dresser?" Kim asked.

"Come look. It's full of wonderful creations. I believe they are all hand made. Just for this occasion," Katie said.

"I hope not," Kim asserted.

"Why?" Katie questioned.

"It all seems real spooky to me," Kim said.

"There you go again. Just go with it," Katie admonished.

"Promise me if things start to get weird, you will just do what I say and not argue. Don't forget what Officer Lopez told us we need to be aware of our surroundings. Right now I don't feel real safe."

"Yes, dear, as long as you are not exaggerating. I want to get into that wonderful dress. It looks simply marvelous," Katie said as she caressed the fabric.

"I'll bet you'll look elegant. What a stunning beauty, that dress. What can I say. Can we just go to bed or, better yet, can I have you on the floor right now?" Kim said half teasing, half serious and completely aroused.

"Please, you're being silly. Our hostesses are waiting. We can pick this up later."

"I don't know if I can wait till later," Kim said as she allowed her eyes to travel the length of her lover.

"Hold that thought, baby. I promise we'll get back to this but for now let's have a glass of wine," Katie suggested.

They poured a glass each to take to the main house. They left the casita fire still burning, sweet smells wafting through the room. It was very dark outside. Kim could hear the howls of stray dogs in the distance.

The pathway to the house was well marked with rocks. They followed it to the front door. It was open, so they entered finding a large Mexican hacienda with traditional Mexican furniture. The hardwood floors creaked as they walked into the great room.

Across the room was a very grand fireplace ablaze with hot wood. The smell of burning hardwood permeated the room. Kim also recognized a familiar smell, the same one she had experienced while taking the shower with Katie. It was very distinct and alluring. They moved slowly towards the warmth of the fire.

"Good evening," a voice came from behind them. It was Juliette. "My you two look enchanting and sexy."

"Yes, Juliette, thanks to your wonderful taste in clothes," Katie said with a smile of appreciation.

"Ladies, if the bodies were not suited for the cloth to drape, one would not notice your beauty," Juliette assured her guests.

"Juliette, you are too kind," again it was Katie who spoke as Kim remained silent and watchful.

"Ladies, come and sit. Dinner in the Mexican tradition is very slowly consumed. It is a happening, a feast to be lavished upon one's guests."

"I do hope we're not intruding upon you and Sera," Kim finally spoke.

"Of course not. We love to entertain, especially the likes of the two of you. It is our pleasure. It will be your pleasure very soon. Let's toast to fine food, wine, and love," Juliette said mysteriously.

Their glasses sparkled in the fire light. As they raised them, Juliette reached over to Katie, and looped her arm around Katie's as she drew the smaller woman into her body and sipped from her glass of wine.

Sera did the same to Kim. Kim could feel Sera's warmth caressing the wine as she sipped the liquid ever so slowly, lingering as long as she could with Kim's arm resting against her full breast. Kim felt very strange. They hardly knew these women yet they seemed to be so close. They released one another sliding back into the large leather sofa, each silent for a moment gazing into one another's eyes as they flickered with the flames of the fire bouncing and jumping.

"Juliette your house is wonderful. So warm and inviting. The casita is just great. I feel as if we have been here a lifetime," Katie offered.

"Ladies, maybe you have. The spirits have a way to offer back a time and place for all of us to meet and return after we leave this earth," Juliette said.

"Juliette, you believe we all have known one another in a previous life?" Kim questioned.

"You tell me. After we have spent this wonderful time together, you will be able to tell me. I must go and get our first course. Please excuse us. Sera, come please. Help yourselves to more of the liquid of the goddesses."

"Katie, remember if things get strange, we need to leave. I think we are involved in something we may regret later," Kim warned her lover.

"Kim, stop being silly. We've had stranger things happen at the Inn. Remember two days ago?"

"Maybe I am being overly sensitive. The recent events at home have made me edgy. We are far away and in another country."

"I will take care of you...don't stress...just enjoy the company," Katie attempted to reassure her.

Juliette and Sera returned with arms full of lovely dishes, Talavera from the interior of Mexico. Each dish was painted with bold prints and deep colors. The women placed the sumptuous delights on the large wooden carved coffee table in front of their guests. Juliette sat next to Katie on the leather sofa.

Sera chose a place next to Kim.

Juliette reached for a piece of tortilla, which she dipped into the cheese and cactus mixture. The cheese ran down and over her fingers as she gently moved the food toward Katie's slightly open lips. Juliette's fingers pushed against Katie's mouth forcing her to allow a finger to enter her mouth. Katie sucked the dripping cheese from the fingers as Juliette gently stroked the inside of Katie's lips while she consumed the tasty bits.

"Was that good?" asked Juliette.

"Yes, I want more. It was intoxicating, so soft and smooth. Katie gazed at Juliette, almost begging Juliette to place her fingers against her soft lips.

If this is the first course, Kim wondered, what would be in store for them with at least five more yet to come. Sera leaned forward reaching across Kim, brushing oh so swiftly against her breasts. Kim felt her nipples tighten as a chill passed through her body.

"Kim?" Sera asked. "Are you cold? You seem to be chilled."

"You noticed, Sera?"

"Yes, of course."

Sera rose from the sofa to add more wood to the fire. Her slim body glistened in the firelight as she bent slowly toward the fireplace opening. Kim almost thought she would be consumed by the flames. Sera reached for a

Mexican woven blanket hanging on the leather chair. She tucked the blanket around Kim's shoulders. She ran her hands across them, stroking the nape of Kim's neck as she snuggled close to keep her warm.

Juliette in a sudden burst of energy leaped to her feet. "My lovely ladies, I think it's time for us to visit the wine making room before we continue with dinner."

Katie, in an emphatic gesture, agreed, and grabbed Kim's hand. She knew Kim wouldn't be as willing to venture to an unknown place hidden away from the rest of the world. Sera gently placed her soft hands on Kim's back urging her to follow Juliette and Katie.

Reluctantly Kim followed the group. Leaving the warmth of the great room behind they walked down a long hall dotted with Mexican art. The collection was most likely worth millions of dollars. Kim wondered how the small winemaker and her girlfriend could possibly amass such a fortune.

Mexico is full of drug dealers. Could our hostesses be involved in drug trafficking? Does she know the Delmonte family and their dark daughter? Have we been drugged? Will we be drugged?

Kim wondered even as she noted that Katie didn't seem at all apprehensive. She seemed to believe they weren't in any danger. The reality was they were in the middle of nowhere, no one knew where they were and it was very dark outside.

I guess Katie figures 'What the hell'...all we can do is enjoy whatever happens and hope for the best.

They reached what seemed to be the end of the long hallway. Juliette unlocked a grand door leading to what appeared to be a basement. She lit a candle and told them to watch their step. The staircase was very old and narrow. Juliette led with Katie and Kim between the two women. Sera still had her hand pressed gently against Kim's back. They finally reached the bottom of the stairs. Juliette circled the large room, lighting what seemed to be hundreds of candles. What appeared to be a large round spa-like barrel was in the center of the room. It looked like an oak barrel. Surrounding the barrel were claw foot bathtubs. Kim counted four. Juliette escorted them toward the large barrel.

"My ladies, this is where we make our wine." They peered over the edge of the barrel to find whole grapes at the bottom. "As you know we call our winery Three Women's Winery. "

Katie asked, "Why three?"

"You will see in time, my love. Be patient. Are you ready to join in some wine making?" Juliette asked.

Katie and Kim looked at one another.

"Please, it is the most sensuous experience you will ever have. Sera and I will prepare you for the wine celebration. Please come over here. You must take off your clothes. We will then bathe you in the tubs, washing you clean of any unwanted scents and oils from your previous bath," Juliette said.

I wonder if all the other guests who helped in the women's wine making also experienced this treatment. Somehow I don't think they had the pleasure. These women are on a mission with us along for the ride, Kim thought.

"Juliette, I'm not sure I am ready to make wine," Kim said.

"Kim, you have done this many times before. You just have no memories"

"I know I'm Italian, but naked in a wine barrel, never," Kim replied.

"I can assure you, you will in time have those memories. Please trust me, Kim. Please let me pour you a glass of wine. It will relax you."

Sera and Juliette took them over to a small sitting area with fainting couches. In the center of them was a round table with wine glasses, four of them. Juliette selected a bottle of wine from one of several hundred against the room's walls. She seemed to know exactly which bottle she wanted. She did not hesitate to read the labels. Sera seated them on the couches in a reclining position. Juliette poured the wine and handed Katie and Kim their glasses. Sera and Juliette took a position on the carpeted floor next to each one of them.

As they sipped the wine, Kim began to experience the same feeling she had earlier in the day. The room filled with light. It seemed to blur. Sera knelt beside Kim. She took on an almost spiritual appearance. She radiated. She glowed. Her touch was warm against Kim's skin as she stroked her, unbuttoning her blouse and pants. Kim didn't resist.

Her touch is familiar. I know the gentle hands that now stroke me. Could what Juliette said about a past life be right?

⁂

"Katie!" Kim awoke suddenly lying next to the love of her life in the casita. *What a dream I just had. How did we get in this bed? What happened to dinner?*

"Kim, what is wrong with you? I've lost you twice today, once in the wine cave and then again at dinner. We had a fabulous meal. The ladies treated us to more wine and several courses of the best Mexican food I've ever tasted. The fish was out of this world. Juliette prepared it at the dinner table. You seemed to enjoy every last mouthful. I think the wine has gone to your head," Katie explained.

"I don't seem to remember eating or walking back to our casita," Kim replied.

"I think you dreamed most of the evening."

"You mean we didn't go to the wine making room?"

"What? No! It was late. Juliette was nice enough to make dinner. The tour has been postponed for another visit," Katie assured her.

"You mean we are coming back here again to spend the night?" Kim questioned.

"Yes, I just love this place. I wish our Inn had this amount of old world charm and the winery. I would love to own a winery. We need to sleep. We should get an early start in the morning. I told the women we wouldn't bother them when we left. They are early risers and start wine making very early. I told them we would return very soon. Juliette gave me her private phone number. Good night. I love you."

"I love you," Kim replied softly in a still stunned voice.

Katie fell right to sleep but Kim lay awake for hours as she struggled with the questions running through her mind.

Chapter Six

The Long Ride To Playa Blanca

Katie was very quiet as they began the drive back to their condo along the familiar bumpy dirt road from the winery.

"Please don't take the back road to Rosarito Beach," Kim requested. She was still a bit hung over from the night's festivities. The back road was rather desolate and the perfect place to make someone disappear.

"You're just being paranoid. There's no need to worry," Katie assured her partner in her usual tone.

Kim wasn't sure if it was the wine or what might have been added to the lush dark liquid blended by those women, but she felt much more hung over than usual after a night of drinking. The bumpy road did not help her unsettled stomach. They finally reached the paved road and Katie eased forward with caution.

"If you really don't want to go home on the back road we can take the ocean toll road," Katie offered in deference to her partner's discomfort.

"I know you are sweet to ask and I appreciate your concern for me but I know how much you enjoy the country road so let's go for it. I will try and enjoy the scenery." Kim tried not to let Katie know that she would be watching every car and truck within miles of their car.

Katie and Kim had often stopped to enjoy the towns and sights along the route from the winery to their condo but they didn't take time for such pleasures as they sped along the road. They wanted to get back to close up the condo, and then head back to Palm Springs. Although it was tempting to stay longer, they had neglected Darla and their obligations at the hotel long enough. Avoiding the situation they had left behind would not make it go away. The last time they spoke with Darla she had gotten a call from Officer Lopez who told her the department had been following some leads in the case, but none of them panned out. Jill was cooperating with the police and had not heard or received any communications from anyone who might want a ransom. Jill planned to leave the country to finish the film she had started with Trish.

Officer Lopez had expressed concern for Kim and Katie and wanted to make sure nothing had happened to them while in Mexico, especially during their visit to the wine country. Darla informed them that Lopez now suspected that Trish's kidnapping had something to do with them, not Jill. She feared they could be the real targets of whoever abducted Trish from the hotel.

"Katie, you are driving way too slow. Can't you speedup?" Kim complained.

"No, we don't want to get pulled over by the policia. That would not be a good thing. I don't have the bribe money," Katie said.

"Sorry I forgot, must be the wine haze affecting my brain," Kim replied.

"I can pick up some speed when we get through the town. I promise."

"Hey, look over there do you see that guy across the road?"

"Yes, what is he doing?" Katie asked.

"I don't know for sure, but it looks like he is...no can't be...yes, he is selling that gringo dope right out in the open," Kim said in amazement. "That American is flashing lots of money I can see it from here. He doesn't know he's in for a big surprise when he drives away. Katie, let's get out of here."

"Hope he doesn't take the back road with us," Katie said in alarm.

As they reached the end of the town, Kim was looking in her side mirror watching for the man. "What a dumb gringo, pot smoking, cocaine sniffing idiot," she muttered. "Katie, put the pedal to the metal and get us the hell away from here," Kim requested.

The open fields of green grass seemed to stretch for miles. This part of Mexico looked as if no one had ever set foot on the land it was so isolated. They had not gone but a couple of miles when Kim saw a car coming up behind them from out of nowhere. Kim felt anxious as she watched it gaining on them. She didn't say a word to Katie, who seemed to be totally unaware of its approach. Kim's heart raced. Her chest felt as if it would explode. She was sure Katie could see her breasts welling up under the pressure. Kim's breathing became rapid, her hands began to sweat. She was recalling all of the stories she had read about people being car jacked, raped and robbed along the toll road. This was far more secluded than the toll. Kim wanted to scream at Katie but knew that would do no good. If it was nothing, it would cause her unnecessary alarm. Kim waited and continued to watch the car.

Suddenly there it was...in the distance Kim could see a black SUV. She debated whether or not to tell Katie. Instinct told her it was time. They would need to make a plan.

"Katie, I don't want to alarm you but there is a big black SUV behind us. It's been tailing us for about five miles. There is another black SUV in front of us. Do you think this is cause for alarm?"

"I saw the car behind us but didn't think anything of it. Now that we have another one in front of us this might be a problem."

Kim's heart really began to pump. She could feel her blood pressure rising. If Katie was not comfortable, it meant something was wrong.

"I will try my best if they approach, to not stop even if I have to go off-roading. Make sure your seat belt is fastened and hold on. We are really far from civilization. I'm not sure I can out maneuver or out run them. If they pull us over we are toast," Katie said.

"The car behind us is speeding up and they are gaining on us. If you drive faster, we will get closer to that car in front of us."

"Kim, I have to do something."

"Like what? We risk getting hurt no matter what we do. Remember they probably have guns. We have nothing to defend ourselves. I would say to use our cell phones, but the damn things don't get a signal out here, not until we get to La Mission. If we make it that far and I doubt that will happen. If these guys are truly after us, they will make a move very soon," Kim said with a quiver in her voice.

"What if I speed up to try and pass the front car and then make a run for it? This car can hit one thirty or more," Katie said.

"Katie, don't be nuts! Have you forgotten the winding hills coming up? We will be forced off the road over the steep cliff." Kim predicted.

"You're right. I guess we have to take our chances with them. I'll keep coasting along to see what they do," Katie decided.

Kim wanted to protect Katie will all her mind, heart and soul but she knew that the situation could be very serious. Her heart pounded as she watched the SUVs prepare to block them in.

"Katie, are you ready? They are going to box us in. I suggest we let them. If we run, they will become more agitated and aggressive," Kim said with a confidence she didn't really feel.

"I hope they speak English," was Katie's short reply.

"Are you kidding?" Kim asked. "Most of these guys are US citizens working their trade in Mexico where they don't get arrested. What's strange to me is that no one is usually a target unless they have drug ties." Kim added.

As soon as the words were out of her mouth, the SUVs boxed them in.

"Shit. It's over. We're boxed in, Katie. Just stop the car. Let me do the talking," Kim said in a rush.

"Okay, go for it."

Katie brought the car to a stop on the side of the road. They sat very still not knowing if they would be killed, robbed or worse...raped. Kim reached over and held Katie's hand, waiting for the men to approach the car.

Four heavily armed men surrounded the car, yelling in English, as if they knew the women didn't speak Spanish. "Get out of your car now," the apparent leader of the pack yelled at them.

Guns were drawn and pointed at the women's heads. Kim and Katie slowly exited the car with their hands extended into the air.

"What do you want with us?" Kim asked.

One of the men placed his gun at the back of Kim's head and started to push her into the field. Kim thought he was going to kill her right then and there.

"Senor, we have money and you can have our car. Please don't hurt us, we will not tell anyone about you, just let us go," Kim said in a rush.

"Shut up you bitch. Just do what we tell you or we will kill you and toss your bodies in the field for the vultures to feed on you," the man replied in an angry tone.

The other men pushed Katie to the ground and Kim's stomach began to churn and she fought the urge to throw up. *Oh my God. They're going to rape her. Please don't harm her.* Kim had just decided to take her chances and rush them. She was certain it would be better to die trying to protect Katie rather than watching them ravage her. Suddenly she realized they were putting a handkerchief over Katie's eyes. "Stay on the ground," Kim heard them tell her partner.

They then did the same thing to Kim. Once they had her eyes covered, they dragged her over to where they had Katie and pushed her hard to the ground. Kim felt a large foot on her back holding her down. Then she felt the cold hard steel of a gun barrel at the back of her head. She was waiting for everything to go dark as a bullet entered her head but it didn't happen. Kim could hear Katie's heavy breathing. She was scared beyond anything she had ever felt in her life. Neither woman dared to speak or comfort one another for fear of what the men would do to them if they spoke.

"Stay on the ground and do not move. You understand me?" a man spoke right in Kim's ear. She nodded her head that she understood.

"You stay where you are for a half hour and do not move or you will be shot. You understand?" the man questioned again and Kim could feel the heat of his breath on her cheek. Again she nodded her understanding.

After a few minutes the women heard car doors being opened and closed. Then came the blessed sound of the cars starting and pulling away. Kim and Katie stayed still until they were certain the cars had driven off. Kim was the first to pull off her blindfold. She immediately crawled over to Katie.

"It's okay, honey. It's okay. They're gone," Kim whispered to her lover as she pulled the blindfold from Katie's eyes.

Katie began to sob and fell into Kim's arms. The women just held onto each other. Kim stroked Katie's back and placed small kisses on her face and forehead. She used her gentle touch to soothe Katie and give her strength. Once Katie's sobs had subsided, Kim raised up to look around. All she saw was an empty space and not a person in sight.

"Katie let's get up, but slowly. It hasn't been a half hour and they could still be watching us."

Kim attempted to rise to her feet but her legs buckled and she fell to the ground. The strain and emotion of the last hour had obviously taken a toll on her. Katie was already on her feet. She reached out a hand to her lover. She gave a tug and pulled Kim to her feet and straight into her arms. They stood for long moments as they regained their strength and basked in the knowledge that they were alive.

"I think they are gone, Katie, and it looks like we still have our car," Kim said.

"What did they want? Why did they stop us?" Katie asked.

They soon had that answer. On the front seat on the driver's side was a business card. Katie picked up the card and gasped in revulsion at the message that had been written on it in a strong hand.

"Greetings from the one who wants you. TAZ."

Katie handed Kim the card as she collapsed on to the ground beside the car.

Kim felt a fiery rage fill her as she read the card. But she knew the important thing was for them to get on the road and home to safety as quickly as possible. She helped Katie to her feet and once again pulled her lover into the safety of her arms.

"We need to get home, baby. It doesn't look like they took a thing so let's get out of here and find a phone, okay?" Kim asked in a soothing voice.

Kim helped Katie into the passenger seat and she took the wheel.

"I want to get to a phone and call Officer Lopez. We need to tell her what happened and ask for her help to decide what to do," Kim said.

Kim didn't slow down until they reached LA Mission. She quickly located a phone and put in a call to Officer Lopez. She felt a sense of relief as soon as she heard the police officer pick up. Kim relayed their story and asked for guidance.

"I know you're scared, but you need to calm down and get home to the States right away," Officer Lopez said.

Kim listened for a few more minutes as the police officer filled her in on the investigation and once again told her to get out of Mexico and into the United States as quickly as possible.

❧❧❧❧

Kim and Katie decided they couldn't possibly drive straight through to Palm Springs and would need to stop for the night. They decided La Fonda should be safe enough for the night. The hotel was staffed with security and they would park close to the entrance of their room and not venture too far from the hotel until they headed out for home the next morning.

The sun was just beginning to set when they reached the hotel. She managed to get a parking spot right in front of the room right next to the office. She smiled at Katie in relief.

"Come on, honey. Let's get checked in and then find something to eat. I'm suddenly starved," Kim said.

"As crazy as this day has been, I'm hungry too," Katie laughed for the first time in what seemed like forever.

They stepped out of the car and after making sure it was locked, they made their way to the quaint old office and rang the metal bell.

After a few seconds an older Spanish women dressed in a colorful dress greeted them in Spanish and then in English. "Can I help you?" she asked.

Katie requested Room 103 if it was available. They were relieved to learn that it was and the woman soon had them checked in and handed over the room key. They got their overnight bags out of the car and Kim opened the door to the room just as the sun was beginning to sink below the horizon. The room was not fancy, no phone or television. But the space was warm and inviting and they welcomed the safety it would bring.

A few hours earlier they would not have imagined they would be here together preparing to enjoy a nice meal and watch the sun go down as the Mexican skies filled with bright stars in the clear night sky. They could see people sitting at tables on the balcony of the restaurant that abutted the hotel. One loud scream and someone would notice. This is not that deserted stretch of road.

They unpacked the few things they would need for the night in virtual silence. Finally Kim broke the silence. "Katie, lets go outside and watch the sky turn colors. The sun is setting and you know how beautiful the Mexican sky gets as the sun sinks below the horizon. It's safe here so don't worry that any one is going to get us."

The hotel provided a bottle of wine for its guests and Kim placed the wine, two glasses and the opener on a tray to carry with them onto the patio off their room. She set the tray on the table and opened the wine. She filled two glasses and turned to find Katie still standing in th doorway. She picked up the glasses filled with the red liquid and walked to stand in front of Katie. "Here, my love, sip this. I know it will make you feel better."

Katie took the offered glass and brought it to her lips. She sipped and closed her eyes. Kim watched as her lovers tongue slipped out to lick away the remaining wine from her lips. Kim stood as if transfixed, watching Katie's every movement. And when Katie opened her eyes, Kim saw that they were pooling with tears.

Kim gently took the glass from Katie's hand and placed it with her own on the small table provided with each of the oceanfront rooms. Then she stepped close to her lover never once breaking eye contact. Each knew what the other was thinking without words being spoken. They had escaped death that day making the night and coming days even more precious.

Kim reached out a finger and gently traced the shape of Katie's face as she looked down at the woman she loved more than her own life. Katie looked at her with such love and devotion that her eyes began to fill as well.

"I was afraid I was going to lose you," she finally whispered. "Katie, I couldn't stand it if something happened to you. I love you with all that I am. You know that, right?"

"Honey, I have never doubted your love for one instant. Even when I was blindfolded and forced to the ground, I took comfort in knowing that you love me and were close by."

Kim leaned down and gently took Katie's lips with her own. It was a kiss of healing, of love, of commitment and of promise. Katie returned the kiss just as sweetly and wrapped her arms around Kim and settled her body as close to the taller woman as she possibly could. They remained in that position for endless moments until Katie's stomach gave a loud rumble causing them to simultaneously burst into laughter.

"I refuse to let these people have control over our lives, Katie. Let's not allow them to beat us down. I say that we finish our wine and then go next door and have a wonderful meal to celebrate."

"Celebrate?" Katie asked.

"Yes, celebrate that we're here. We're together. And we're alive."

❧❧❧❧

They were seated side by side at a table overlooking the ocean. As the sky turned bright orange and then pink, Katie and Kim sat in silence staring at the ocean and watching the dolphins play. Kim reached out and took Katie's hand in her own. It seemed easier not to speak. Even as they enjoyed the soothing scene before them they were never quite relaxed. They glanced nervously around the restaurant wondering if there was someone there watching, wanting to do them harm.

"Kim, this has to be over. I pray Lopez and her team can make all of this come to an end and quickly."

"I wouldn't place too much hope on Lopez, after all, she is dealing with an international gang. They can do what they want here in Mexico. No one cares as long as they get paid off."

"I know. You're right but I can only hope what

happened can be stopped and those who are doing this can be brought to justice in the United States. If not, I'm afraid we are in for many more scary days in our lovely city across the border."

The waiter placed their food in front of them. Although it had been many hours since either and eaten and Katie's stomach had rumbled earlier, neither managed to eat very much. They moved the food around on their plates but consumed very little of what would normally have been a very delicious meal.

"I won't let that bitch, Taz, ruin our lives or make us fearful of Mexico. I swear I will kill the bitch before she kills me," Kim said with a touch of venom in her voice. "I think we should call Officer Lopez and let her know where we are and perhaps get an update. We need to reclaim control of our lives."

"I agree with you, honey. Let me call her this time and then we'll decide how we proceed from here," Katie replied.

Once Katie got the officer on the phone and identified herself, she did more listening than talking. Kim watched the different emotions play across her lover's face and knew that she wasn't happy with some of the things she was hearing. She waited impatiently for Katie to end the call and fill her in.

"Tell me," Kim said as soon as the call ended.

"First of all, she's upset that we're still in Mexico and warned us to be careful and to get across the border as quickly as possible. It seems that she has been in touch with some Mexican authorities and has some information about the men who stopped us today. She's not one hundred percent certain the information is accurate. If it is, the men have ties to the Delmonte family. They said they are body guards and often escort the family members back and forth to the United States. They also said they may have other ties to the La Familia drug cartel. This cartel is the up and coming powerhouse of cartels in Mexico. They've even been seen hiding drugs inside a blanket wrapped around a baby. They are ruthless according to Officer Lopez." Katie relayed.

"Oh my God. This scares the hell out of me."

The women hardly noticed the beauty of the scene before them. The outside patio was decorated with twinkling lights. Warm beach air wafted off the ocean and stars had begun to sparkle in the night sky. Where once it would have been the perfect backdrop for a night of romance, tonight each sat quietly lost in her own thoughts.

While they sat, music had begun to play in the dance area. Women and men dressed in bright colors much like that of costumed dancers began to move on the dance floor.

"Kim?" Katie finally broke the silence.

"Yes." Kim questioned.

"You're going to think I'm crazy, and maybe I am, but let's go find a quite corner, have a few drinks, listen to the music and watch the dancers," Katie requested.

Kim looked startled for a moment. That was the last thing she expected to hear from Katie after the events of their day. "Are you sure you want to hang out in the bar?"

"I am not afraid. Look at all the people. We will be fine and besides it might make us relax," Katie insisted.

"If you're sure this is what you want to do—"

"Yes, it is," Katie interrupted. "We can sit at that table over there and no one will see us," she said as she gestured to a table in a secluded corner hidden by the shadows.

Once they had claimed the table, Kim looked around. She could see the entire room from her vantage point. The bar was really beginning to fill up and more and more dancers were taking to the floor, moving in rhythm with the music. Drinks were flowing freely and people were quickly losing their natural inhibitions. Women danced with women. Men with men. She saw a dark haired woman who appeared to be in her forties open her blouse and bare her breasts for all to see. Maybe it was the bawdy actions of the woman or the outrageous colors the dancers wore or simply the stress from the day but Kim suddenly found herself bursting out in laughter.

"Oh my God, where do these people come from?" she asked.

Katie looked at her partner and then around them at the dancers. When her eyes fell on the woman's bare chest, she too began to laugh.

Kim found she had the urge to dance and become part of the revelry. She grabbed Katie by the hand and pulled her up and onto the dance floor. They joined the energetic group flailing around the dance floor. For that moment in time, they had not a care in the world. All the worries of the day were forgotten under the beat of the music, the release of the dance.

Then Kim saw her. A dark figure watched them from across the dance floor. "Katie, come with me back to the table right now. Don't look around or make any big gesture."

Katie looked up at Kim with a question in her eyes. But one look at Kim's face told her all she needed to know. Kim had gone white as a sheet.

"Come on, baby. We need to return to our table," Kim urged her partner.

Their feet felt heavy as lead as they made the short walk back to their table. They slid into the tuck and roll booth. Their bodies made squeaking noises as they slid across the vinyl seat. Kim sat close to Katie so she could be heard over the music.

"Katie, look over at the end of the bar. Tell me what you see," she said into her partner's ear.

Katie looked through the hordes of dancers on the floor. Her eyes quickly settled on a dark figure sitting with at drink in hand at the end of long bar and close to the entrance.

"Oh my! Shit, Kim, I think that's —."

"I know. I'm sure it's her," Kim whispered in growing alarm.

"Kim, what do we do now? You know she saw us on the dance floor. Who knows how long she has been sitting at the bar before you spotted her?"

"We have no choice but to stay put. If we want to leave, we would have to walk right by her. I think we should stay here and have another drink. Maybe even dance some more. We can pretend that seeing her here doesn't bother us and maybe she will just go away," Kim said.

"Okay, Kim, we'll stay here and wait her out."

"Don't know about you, but I could use another drink. I'll get the waiter's attention," Kim said.

As if out of nowhere the waiter showed up at her side but not to take their order but to deliver drinks. "The lady at the end of the bar sends you her compliments," he said as he placed the drinks in front of them.

The drinks had smoke billowing from them as the waiter lit them on fire, some sort of a black Russian. They sat stunned as the flames from the drinks illuminated their faces, giving Taz a clear view of the horror on their faces. Kim quickly blew out the flame on her drink and Katie followed suit.

"Katie, this sucks. I want to confront her. I want to ask her what in the hell does she want with us. If we let this go on, she will terrorize us forever. Maybe we should call Lopez," Kim rambled.

"Kim, what good would that do us? She has no jurisdiction here, besides what good is she in Mexico. I sure don't want her to call the local police. They are most likely on Taz's payroll."

"God, you're right. I keep forgetting we're not in the United States. This is her turf, and she manages it very well," Kim said.

"Let's just sit and chill. Maybe she will get tired and go away," Katie said with a hopeful tone.

"No way. She is so excited right now. Like a hawk circling its prey. If I could see her face clearly, I would bet it is overcome with excitement. This is her thing, this is her pleasure. I bet she cannot have real sex; she has to have those so called creatures pleasure her in ways we have never experienced. Remember those words from the night at Toucans? The longer she has us here, the more excited she will become," Kim said in horror.

"God Kim, what an awful thought. I hate to think we are providing her with any gratification at our expense."

"She has been satisfying herself all day. I'm sure she was with those guys this afternoon. The card on the seat was from her, put on the seat by her," Kim said in disgust.

"Damn! Of course, that makes perfect sense. After all we had our faces to the ground; that bitch was probably standing right beside us," Katie said as her anger grew to match her fear.

"I don't know about you, but I refuse to let her turn me into a whimpering, frightened child again," Kim said with strength. To lend affirmation to her words, she grabbed Katie by the hand and once again tugged her onto the dance floor.

A very slow, sensual song was playing and Kim

pulled Katie close in her arms. She turned them so that Katie's back was to their nemesis and only she could see the dark one staring directly at them, her eyes fixed on their every move. Kim stared back as if to say, "I'm not afraid." Taz began to move.

"The bitch is coming toward us. Don't say a word or acknowledge her in anyway. Okay?" Kim whispered in Katie's eye ear. She felt Katie take in a sharp breath and release it as she pulled her more firmly into her arms as if to protect her.

Taz settled a mere two feet away from them on the dance floor and began to sway to the music. Suddenly she released her signature black cape and tossed it to the floor, revealing a skimpy lace top and a very short skirt. Her long slender legs were clearly visible below the skirt, beautiful and tan. Her breasts were large and full, protruding above the tank top. Her long black hair fell just above her chest, dark and pronounced as it cascaded over her bronze skin. Her face was chiseled with striking features, erotic, almost intoxicating. Taz's eyes seemed magical, deep dark brown surrounded by billowing eye lashes. If she were not an evil person, this beauty would be desired by anyone who saw her.

Katie and Kim stared in stunned fascination as they continued to hold onto one another. Taz feared nothing as she glided forward, inching closer, eyes fixed on the women. The other patrons in the bar watched the spectacle unfolding in front of them. All eyes were glued to the woman, captivated by her beauty as she commanded the entire room.

Taz stopped just short of the two women. A glow coated her skin as if she was bathed in oils. She was perfection, drenched in shimmering light, not a flaw on her body. Taz stood motionless making eye contact with Kim and Katie, almost an innocent gaze, not that of a person who earlier that day had tried to kill them. Kim and Katie stepped back a few steps distancing themselves from her. They could feel her cool breath. It was almost sweet, the scent of a rich fine wine. Then out of the darkness came another figure moving towards the three women.

Kim was afraid this could be the person who might help Taz escort the two of them from the bar. Kim pulled Katie even tighter into her embrace. Kim squeezed back as it to say it would be okay.

The scantily clothed figure approached Taz from behind. They could not tell if it was a man or woman. They were as striking as Taz. Tall...slender...wearing black, skin tight jeans and a well fitted black tank top that revealed very small, well formed breasts. Arms long with defined muscles, not large but sleek. The two stood motionless, bodies entwined, for a long moment. Their eyes locked on Katie and Kim. They did not speak or move. And then the music changed. It became strong a pounding beat. The two beautiful creatures started to move to the pulse of the music. Many Mexican musical groups dedicate much of their songs to illustrate darker parts of their culture. The songs are played to evoke deep feelings and emotions. Taz and her companion treated the patrons to a performance unlike any they had ever seen. The two were one body as they melted into one another and began to move on the dance floor. Taz glided her hands over the second dancer as if she were stroking each and every inch available to her.

"Katie, we should get out of here while they are dancing. This is the perfect time," Kim whispered.

But before they could make their get away, the lights went out leaving the dance floor in complete darkness. The only illumination in the room came from the flickering candles on the tables scattered about the room. Kim and Katie found themselves unable to see across the bar. They lost sight of the two figures in the darkness. Kim stayed close to Katie with her hand on the small of Katie's back. Kim stiffened as she felt it and Katie let out an involuntary breath of alarm... a hand on each of their shoulders was there for an instant and then it was gone as were the dancers.

Her heart racing, Kim tugged on Katie's hand and pulled her toward the entrance. "Let's get out of here and back to our room," Kim said.

Once they were safely inside, they made a quick survey to be sure no one had entered and was hiding within. Then they pushed the large dresser in front of the door, adrenalin racing. Kim's eyes darted around the room and stopped on the large sliding door to the patio. They had no way of protecting themselves from that window.

"Kim, don't worry about the glass door. It is a very steep cliff that cascades down to the sand and ocean below. No one can make it up that cliff without ropes. I'm sure Taz is gone for the night," Katie assured her partner.

Before settling in for the night, they made one last call to Officer Lopez to fill her in on their latest incident with Taz and her "twin."

Chapter Seven

The Border Crossing

They got an early start back to their condo and quickly had it taken care of and were ready to make the drive to the border. On a good day the drive from their condo to the crossing would take about forty-five minutes. Kim estimated they would reach the San Yseido soon after eleven o'clock. The roads were relatively quiet. Only the usual cars heading for a shopping trip in San Diego joined them on the road.

They reached the Sentri lanes and started through the border checkpoint. They took out their Sentri, trusted travelers' cards and held them up to the scanner and waited for the agent to wave them up. Suddenly out of the corner of her eye, Kim saw a patrol agent with his drug sniffing dog approaching the car. The dog began sniffing the rear of the car and hit on their car. The patrolman instructed Kim to pull over to the secondary checkpoint on the other side of the gate. The officer along with the dog followed them to the appropriate parking spot.

"Will you ladies step out of your car, please?" he asked.

A slew of questions followed. The agents wanted to know where they had been. If they had left the car unattended. They watched in horror as the agent slid under the car and and pulled out a bag of white powder that had been sealed to the car with duct tape. He repeated the action four more times. Each time he slid out with another bag of powder in his hand.

Another agent opened one of the bags and revealed what appeared to be cocaine to their shocked eyes. Police surrounded them and one of the female officers approached them. "Put your hands behind your backs, please," she said politely but with authority. Once they were cuffed, she left them in the custody of one of the male officers.

It suddenly became clear to Kim and Katie that they were in big trouble and why they had been stopped out in the deserted field. That is why they were not killed or hurt. They needed them to transport the cocaine across the border. And that's why they followed them to La Fonda, they were watching their stash and had to make them so afraid that they would leave the country, head back to Palm Springs with the drugs.

"Katie, we have got to call Lopez. We are going to be arrested. She needs to explain to these people what has been happening the last two days," Kim said in alarm.

"Officer can you wait, please? We can explain all of this if you will just speak to the officer in Palm Springs. She can explain why we have had drugs planted in our car," Katie implored.

The border patrol officer was a big ugly fat man and Kim doubted he would listen to them. He soon proved her correct.

"Sure, lady, we have heard every story. Yours is just another lie to stop us from throwing your sorry druggie asses in jail with all the rest of the dykes," he said with a snarl. Kim and Katie looked at one another, the image of being in a dirty jail cell with drug dealers made them even sicker than they were in that field with those scary men.

The female officer approached them again and

walked straight up to the big guy.

"Take the cuffs off of them, now," she instructed.

"What for?" he asked with a surprised look. "These dykes are going to the tank."

"Back off," the woman warned. "I will take care of them. You go find something else to do."

Much to their surprise and relief he did as she asked and then turned and walked away but they still heard the words he muttered just under his breath. "Damned bull dykes, all three of them."

"Thank you," Kim offered.

"Not a problem. Come with me please," the officer instructed.

They were led to a small room with a few very uncomfortable chairs scattered about. Better than a jail cell. "You have a seat and I'll be back soon," the officer said as she turned and left the room.

"Katie, they probably want to haul a whole bunch of us at one time. This is the waiting room. I would guess we will be joined by our fellow drug smugglers shortly. Maybe a few more dykes. This may be the occupation of choice for a few of us?"

"Be serious," Katie reprimanded her.

"I am." Kim replied.

They mostly sat in silence. Each lost in her own thoughts. But the waiting soon took its toll on Kim. "I'm tired of waiting. What are they doing? Why can't they just do whatever they're are going to do and end this?" Kim asked in exasperation.

They heard voices coming toward the door.

"Maybe they're coming for us," Katie whispered.

"Maybe they're bringing in more drug smugglers," was Kim's tart reply.

The door opened slowly. To their surprise and

tremendous relief, Officer Lopez walked in accompanied by the officer. They jumped to their feet and threw themselves into the officer's arms. Surprised she embraced both of them.

"We are so happy to see you. How did you find us?" Katie asked in a rush.

"What is going on? Are we going to jail? They found cocaine in our car," Kim added.

"Slow down," the officer instructed. "You were very easy to find. After I talked to you yesterday and you told me you were not coming home but stopping at La Fonda, I made some fast phone calls to the police I knew I could trust in Mexico. I had a hunch the mugging attempt in the wine country was suspicious. What you experienced there just doesn't fit the normal MO for that type of attack. When I made contact with the powers that be, they told me a gang headed by the Delmonte Family was smuggling high quality cocaine into the States using mules who were beautiful, white women. They were putting the drugs in their cars, buying off the U.S. Border Patrol agents at the gate and smuggling millions of dollars of dope into our country," she explained.

"Oh my God!" Katie exclaimed.

"They distribute to very high end clients. I mean very high end. The stuff they found in your car is worth millions of dollars. It is the purest of pure...the caviar of cocaine. That is why you were being followed and made to feel you had to get to the United States fast. After I spoke to you last night, I called the FBI. They have been collaborating with us on this case. I told them the events that had taken place on the road from the wine country. They had been planning on meeting with us to tell us the new evidence they had uncovered leading to the disappearance of Trish and her connection to the drug dealers, Taz, her family and

Jill. The pieces to the Trish kidnapping were beginning to fall into place after the FBI spoke to us. I knew I had to move fast to put the facts together."

"What did they find out about Trish?" Katie asked.

"That was one of the reasons I was so worried about you," Officer Lopez replied. "Trish is why I insisted you return to the United States immediately," the officer paused before she continued. "Trish's body was found in a garbage dump outside of Tijuana."

Both women gasped in horror and shock as the color faded from their faces.

"Oh my God! That's horrible. How did they find her?" Katie finally asked.

"Trish's body was found by some homeless kids who have been abandoned to live on the streets. They were scavenging through the trash looking for food when they came across her body. Trish suffered a horrible death. Her body was mutilated. She paid dearly for no longer being useful to the drug cartel. They made sure they took back everything they had helped her attain...her beauty, her eyes. I've rarely heard of anything like it. Her breasts were cut off, her eyes gouged out. We believe it was an execution...a ritual killing of punishment. We think there may have been many who watched her suffering and eventual death," Officer Lopez explained.

"That's horrible," Katie said as tears began to fill her eyes. Kim moved closer to her partner and put an arm around her shoulders. "Kim, that could've been us!"

"But it wasn't. We're here and we are safe," she assured her partner before turning to the police officer. "One thing I don't understand is why us? Why did we get stopped if they pay off the gate agents? How did they know we would choose the correct lane? There are five lanes to choose from."

"Very goods questions, Kim. After Trish was out of commission, you can guess, the FBI thought she was running drugs for high end clients. We had not connected the dots. When Trish could no longer provide the delivery service, Taz found the two of you who fit the profile. You make frequent trips to Mexico, bam! You were it. I don't believe she planned to use you forever. She needed to move this particular load of coke. Her clients were going to switch to another source if she did not deliver," Officer Lopez explained.

"How did she know we were going to Mexico in time to bring the drugs back?" Katie asked.

"You told her in the bar the night she ran into you, Katie. I am sure Trish also convinced Taz you two would be perfect in an effort to get herself off the hook. More dots connected."

"Shit you are right I did mention Mexico. I am so dumb, way too much information," Katie said in self-disgust.

"Don't kick yourself. You didn't know. She followed you every step of the way from the time you left Palm Springs to the time you fell into her hands. Going to the wine country, taking the deserted road home, it was perfect," Officer Lopez added.

"Think it worked," Kim mumbled under her breath.

"The other person you mentioned that Taz had with her? We are not sure who that could be. I believe it is a double that Taz uses to throw the police off. We never know exactly who it is we are following. The question about the border gate? That is actually very simple. I am sure you didn't notice anyone walking around your car while you waited in line. Someone who appeared to be selling something. There are so many street vendors selling stuff while you wait to cross. A car cutting in front of you making you change lanes forcing you over. It happened. It was so smooth you didn't notice. We knew what was going down, we knew which gate they had chosen. Thanks to some really good FBI and ICE investigative work, we found the agent who was on the take, replaced him with a good guy and voila. We had the dog sniffing cop intercept your car prior to your arrival at the gate. The officer at that gate then told you to go to secondary for further inspection. I am sorry I could not take the chance and tell you what was going on. It would not have been safe for you to know. Not with the kind of drugs you were carrying, worth so much money to the dealers," Officer Lopez completed her explanation.

"Now what? Are we safe? Is this over?" Kim asked. "We botched a drug delivery worth tons of money. I don't think Taz is going to be very happy about this."

"Taz believes you got busted by the police. She knows you didn't have a clue about what you were carrying or you would have not crossed the border. You'd have called me to come to the condo. You would never have stopped at La Fonda if you knew. She knows it wasn't your fault. You did not set her up. It was a botched job. She chose the wrong mules to carry her stuff. Shows her not to mess with good people. Here's what I think. Taz is done with you two. You've been caught. She knows we are watching you. Not worth the risk to plant anything on either of you. In fact, it would be really stupid of her to do anything to you. We would be all over her even in Mexico. Taz is not going to bother you again. We will continue to follow leads that tie her group to the drug trade and money laundering in the states. We are sure many of the dollars went to movies Trish starred in.

"Does that mean Jill is involved?" Kim asked.

"We don't know right now. The FBI still needs to

investigate her connection. My gut feeling, Jill is too much about Jill to ask how Trish got her money. Just give it to me no questions asked. Might be guilt by association. We needed Trish. We have a very weak case against anyone without Trish. Unless we have more trouble with the two of you, we may just close this case and move on," the officer said.

"How can you be sure Trish wasn't just an innocent victim?" Katie asked.

"Katie, we now have enough evidence that links Trish to drug activity to know she was part of it. Trish became too much of a risk to herself and the cartel. Trish was a drug dealer, the worst kind. She played with the big boys and girls. That weekend at your hotel, Taz came for her. They knew it had to look like a kidnapping in order for Jill to finish her film and collect the insurance money for production interruption. Jill could then pay royalties to Taz's clients who had supplied Trish and Jill's company with the production money to make the films," Officer Lopez replied.

"I see why you are not done with Jill and her company," Kim said.

"That's correct, Kim, this warrants further investigation. Let the FBI continue this case. We are done with the kidnapping, but not the murder. I am confident, however, that you two can go about your life without the fear of ever encountering Taz or any of her pals. You are off limits," she said with certainty.

Chapter Eight

Home At Last

Kim and Katie arrived back at the hotel. After checking in with Darla to let her know they were back, they went straight to their rooms. Exhausted and in need of some uninterrupted rest, they stretched out on their bed fully clothed. They only planned to take a short nap before resuming the duties of the hotel but once Katie had settled into the safety of Kim's arms, they slept soundly.

Peace would soon return to their little slice of paradise. They wouldn't allow anyone to interfere with this beautiful place...a bit of heaven on earth for all those who have slept inside its gates. People have stayed on the property since 1932 and guests of the Rainbow Inn have experienced their essence on several occasions. Those spirits will watch over Katie and Kim and keep them safe from any evil that comes their way.

About the Author

My Partner, who comes from the hotel industry, and I are co-owners of an all women's resort in Palm Springs. We moved to the desert almost fourteen years ago from our home in Manhattan Beach, California. At that time, I held a full time job as vice president of sales for the leading supplier of software applications to the apparel industry for retailers and manufacturers. My background in sales and marketing came from owning my own apparel company in the 1970s. I climbed the corporate ladder and had a very successful career for more than twenty-five years.

I spent my early days after high school and during college as a nun and teacher. After leaving the convent, I embarked on another career using my musical talents. I performed in several singing groups and all girl bands when it was not fashionable to be a girl drummer. I come from a musical family, and my father and grandfather were both drummers.

The hotel has a wine cellar, which is an entertainment club where you can occasionally find Donna and me entertaining the hotel guests. Donna is a wonderful singer, song writer and guitar player, while I am the hotel's resident artist and baker.